Do You Believe in
Life After Death?

To David

Happy Reading

Ashley Hernandez

Do You Believe in
Life After Death?

Ashley Harrold

Copyright © 2016 by Ashley Harrold.

Library of Congress Control Number: 2016906498
ISBN: Hardcover   978-1-5144-9860-6
               Softcover   978-1-5144-9859-0
               eBook   978-1-5144-9858-3

All rights reserved. No part of this book may be reproduced or transmitted in any form or by any means, electronic or mechanical, including photocopying, recording, or by any information storage and retrieval system, without permission in writing from the copyright owner.

This is a work of fiction. Names, characters, places and incidents either are the product of the author's imagination or are used fictitiously, and any resemblance to any actual persons, living or dead, events, or locales is entirely coincidental.

Any people depicted in stock imagery provided by Thinkstock are models, and such images are being used for illustrative purposes only.
Certain stock imagery © Thinkstock.

Print information available on the last page.

Rev. date: 04/28/2016

To order additional copies of this book, contact:
Xlibris
800-056-3182
www.Xlibrispublishing.co.uk
Orders@Xlibrispublishing.co.uk
737564

CHAPTER ONE

Hamwell police station at 2 a.m. is a soulless establishment. Viewing it from the outside, the only thing that distinguishes it from any other large Victorian house is a blue light shining brightly above a slightly-larger-than-normal front door. Climbing the four steps and walking through the front door, one is immediately taken aback by the size of the interior. The interior walls, without exception, are of a two-tone brown and yellow. A little arched fireplace stands in one corner of reception. Central heating has rendered it redundant a good many years ago, although it still bears the black scars of raging fires long since extinguished. One can imagine bobbies returning from their beats on cold winter nights, standing in front of it, warming their backsides, the fireplace welcoming them back like an old friend. With just three personnel manning the fort this Tuesday night, it is as quiet as a church mouse; the slightest noise resounds from wall to wall, echoing its way down the single corridor that supplies access to the various offices.

DI Martin Penn is the senior of the two detectives on duty, with ten years' service as a DI. Aged forty-six and showing the first signs of greying hair, he is sitting at his desk, working at his case reports. It is not a job he relishes, but early morning with no distractions is, without doubt, the best time to tackle what he considers to be the most boring aspect of his work. His nicotine fingers plonk away at his laptop. He pauses for a moment. He leans back on his chair, putting his hands on the back of his head, looking down at a packet of Benson & Hedges. He decides to stop for a cigarette. The only plus about working at this ungodly hour is there is nobody to tell him to go outside if he fancied a drag. After reading his report, he decides that he has spent more than enough time on it—another drunken driver, another lamp post needs replacing. 'Christ! When will something interesting happen in this bloody town?' he utters to himself. Taking an old coffee cup and using it as an ashtray, he digs out his notes and continues to write up another case. His partner, Dave Harris, has been recently promoted and has been coupled with Martin for an interim until he finds his feet. Unlike Martin, who has been worn down by years of dealing with the dregs of society, Dave is the young buck, eager to make a name for himself. Martin's impression of his young prodigy is that he is too immature to hold the position of DI, but he is holding it, and so he will just have to live with it. The third person on duty this Tuesday is Sergeant Jack Evans. With twenty-two years' service under his belt, he has accepted he is not going to rise any higher in rank and, at fifty-nine years old, is quite content to see out the rest of his time as desk sergeant at Hamwell police station.

Jack was sat at his desk with his left elbow leaning on the desk, supporting his head, with his right hand holding a pencil, hovering over a crossword puzzle. It was so quiet that the sound of the phone ringing startled Jack for a second. He then picked up the phone.

'Hamwell police station, Sergeant Evans speaking.'

Jack listened to the person on the other end of the phone in disbelief, interrupting at times, commenting, 'No! Never! If this is a hoax—'

Do You Believe in Life After Death?

Finally, he asked for the caller's name and address. He recorded the time of the call then strolled over to Martin's office.

'Martin, I have just taken a strange phone call—apparently someone has been spotted digging up a grave in Hamwell cemetery. I would normally have treated it as a hoax call, but as the caller was prepared to leave his name and address, I thought it needed following up.'

'Okay, Jack, leave it with me,' he said, feeling a little relieved that he had something positive to do.

Martin opened his drawer and cleared his desk. He locked the drawer, something he always did out of habit. He walked to his office door and took his coat off the peg, then strolled down the corridor to Dave's office. He opened the door. Dave was busy playing on his mobile. Martin tut-tutted to himself. *What is the fascination with these phone games?* he thought to himself. 'Put that away, Dave, we have got a call.'

Dave grabbed his black leather jacket and followed Martin out of the station. 'Where are we going, mate?' he asked. If there was one thing that got right up Martin's nose, it was being called *mate*.

'My name is Martin, not mate, and I will explain on the way,' Martin explained where they were going.

They pulled up outside the main gate of the cemetery at 2.45 a.m. With no access into the cemetery for vehicles, they proceeded on foot through the gate.

As cemeteries go, this one was a little larger than most. The two officers sauntered up and down the gravelled path. Dave, who, if truth was known, was not at all at ease in a cemetery at 3 a.m., tried covering his nerves by cracking jokes about ghosts and ghouls. It didn't fool his partner; Martin could read him like a book. They were just about to call it a false alarm, when they heard the sound of metal clashing against stone.

'Did you hear that, Dave? Do you think it's the dead going for their nightly walk around the cemetery?' the senior of the two detectives whispered.

3

'Yes, I bloody did, Martin,' he whispered back. 'It sounds like it's coming from the far corner over there.'

'It's probably an old tramp, Dave. Come on, let's check it out. If we creep up slowly, using the headstones for cover, we can catch whoever it is by surprise.'

'I am right behind you, Martin.' Dave replied, still thinking about the walking dead.

They both slipped from headstone to headstone until they were almost at the scene of the disturbance. They gave it a short time to assess what was happening before moving in. Shining their torches down a big hole in the ground that was once a grave, they saw a young man staring into the torchlight. He was probably in his mid twenties, and was holding a sack. The coffin had been prised open, and he was getting ready to exit the grave.

'Well, Dave, we've got Burke. All we need now is Hare. Come on, son, out you get. Give me your hand, and I will help you up.'

The man took Martin's hand and was lifted to the surface. 'So what have we here then?' asked Martin, taking the old sack from the man's muddy hand. Tipping the contents out, they were quite taken aback by what fell out.

'Wow! It looks like we have hit the jackpot, Dave,' Martin gasped.

A stash of gold and silver items lay before their feet.

'My, my, you have been a naughty boy,' said Dave, who then began to read him his rights. They gathered up the evidence, bundled their prisoner into the squad car, and returned swiftly back to the station. Both officers were feeling more than a little pleased with their night's work. Back at the station, they escorted their prisoner to the front desk, plonked the sack on it, and asked Jack to book him in for the night.

'Name?' said Jack.

'Graham, sir, Graham Peters.'

'Address?'

'In Portsmouth sir, at 72 Marina Close.'
'That's ninety miles away. I mean, where do you live locally?'
'I don't, sir.'
'Are you telling me you have travelled ninety miles to dig up a grave and retrieve a hoard of gold and silver?'
'Yes, sir.'

Jack finished booking him in then offered Graham a little advice. 'Look here, son,' he said in a kind of fatherly way, 'you seem like a decent lad to me. You must realise that you have landed yourself in a heap of trouble. When you are interviewed in the morning, I recommend that you come clean and tell the officers who you stole the gold from.'

'Thanks for the advice, sir,' said Graham. 'That is exactly what I intend to do. But first I must say that I didn't steal it, and the only thing I have done wrong is to disturb a one-hundred-year-old grave.'

Jack was a little surprised by his reply but continued his well-rehearsed duties, telling Graham he would be spending the night as a guest of her majesty and would be interviewed in the morning.

CHAPTER TWO

Len Brown finished reading the police report on the arrest of his client. Mr Peters had been apprehended at 3.30 a.m., after he had just dug up a grave and retrieved a substantial amount of gold and silver from said grave. When asked where he got it all from, he replied it wasn't his. Len closed the folder and wondered why his client hadn't come clean; after all, he had been caught 'bang to rights', as the saying goes. Nevertheless, it was his responsibility to advise him on his best course of action. He returned the folder to the detective in charge and made his way to the interview room, where Graham was sitting facing the two detectives.

He tapped on the door of the interview room. Martin Penn opened it.

Mr Brown introduced himself: 'Len Brown, solicitor for Mr Graham Peters.'

Martin did the introductions. 'My colleague DI Dave Harris. I am DI Martin Penn, and this is your client, Mr Graham Peters.' Len immediately asked the two officers for a few moments alone with his client. 'That suits me,' said Dave. 'I could do with a coffee.'

Martin agreed, adding that he had been on duty since 10.30 last night and was parched.

'As I said, Graham, my name is Len Brown, and I am here to defend you. Anything you tell me is in the strictest confidence, right? Let's get started. Tell me if what I read is true. You were apprehended at 3.30 a.m. in Hamwell cemetery. You dug up a grave and retrieved a substantial amount of gold and silver from a coffin—is that correct?'

'Yes, sir.'

'Please, Graham. Call me Len.'

His first impression of Graham was that he didn't appear to resemble the usual run-of-the-mill low-life criminal that he usually had the misfortune of defending.

'When did you put the stash in the grave?'

'I didn't.'

'Okay, how did you know it was there?'

'You won't believe me if I tell you.'

'Try me.'

'I dreamt it was there.'

'I am afraid you will have to do better than that if we are to keep you out of jail.'

'But it's the truth. I said you wouldn't believe me.'

'Look, Graham, if we go into court, and when the prosecution asks how you knew the valuables were in the grave and you reply you dreamt they were there, we would be made a laughing stock—can you not see that?'

Graham laughed. 'I suppose you're right,' he conceded.

The door opened before Len could continue. Martin and Dave entered. 'Right, let's get on with it,' Martin said rather impatiently, and the four men took to their seats.

Dave read out the charge: 'We will be charging you, Graham Peters, at this junction in time with the desecration of a grave, and being in the possession of what we believe to be stolen goods. I am sure other charges will follow.'

Len interrupted, 'I shall advise my client to make no comment at this moment in time, even at this early stage. There are one or two things I need to clear up in my head first.'

'What might they be?' Dave replied impertinently, as though Len was questioning their detective skills.

'Well, to start with, how did the loot get into the grave? Then has the grave been reported disturbed before? If not, how old was the grave? These are questions I want answered.'

Martin spoke next. 'We deal in facts here, *Mister* Brown, and the facts are as my colleague has just read out.'

'*Mister* Brown,' Len picked up on the emphasis put on the word *Mister. My word I have ruffled someone's feathers,* he thought to himself.

He was used to dealing with detectives and their bullying and aggressive moods. It didn't bother him, but what did bother him was their reluctance to see past the obvious.

Martin stood up, resting both hands on the table and leaning forward directly into Graham's face, asked the question, 'Well, Mr Peters, if you didn't put the loot in the grave, then who did? Who is your accomplice?'

The answer he received rather surprised him.

'First, let me state I am not a common thief. Secondly, what I told you before is the God's honest truth—I did dream it was in that grave. Thirdly, I have a story to tell which I can barely believe, so what you make of it, God only knows, but I feel you must hear it before you condemn me. And lastly, gentlemen, I understand you have been on duty all night and my story will take a long time to explain. In fairness to all parties, may I suggest we postpone this interview until you are a little less tired?'

Dave spoke first. 'Well, thank you very much for your consideration, but I think *we* will determine when this interview concludes.'

Martin, however, was beginning to have the same doubts as Len creep into his mind. 'I, for one', he said, 'am exhausted, and if Mr

Peters has something relevant to say regarding this crime, then I am quite prepared to arrange another interview at a later date. Let's say Friday morning at 10 a.m. Will that be all right with you, Len? You do realise, Graham, we will have to keep you locked up until then.'

'That's fine by me, because when I ask you to verify my story, you will know I haven't been able to cover my tracks. Just one other thing. Could you phone my mother and inform her of my situation?'

'Certainly,' said Martin. 'Write down her phone number, and I will do it right away.'

Dave escorted Graham back to the cells, leaving Martin and Len talking in the interview room. 'What do you make of him, Martin?' Len asked, scratching his head.

'Well, Len, let me first apologise for the way I snapped at you earlier. I think perhaps you are right. There are questions to be answered.'

'What do we actually know about him, Martin?'

'Well, not a lot really. He seems well educated, considerate, likes digging up graves in the middle of the night, and that is about all. Excuse me for a moment, Len. He asked me to phone his mother. Maybe she can throw some light on his behaviour.'

Len thought about leaving but, in the end, decided to wait until Martin returned from his phone call. He inserted fifty pence into the coffee vending machine. A cup of brown water came out, but at least it was hot. Dave bulldozed into the room, ranting. 'That client of yours has got more front than Sainsbury's.' Len stayed silent. He was already forming an opinion of Dave, and it was not particularly flattering.

CHAPTER THREE

The phone rang. A smartly dressed, well-spoken lady in her midfifties picked up the receiver. On hearing a man's voice, she immediately assumed it was her son. 'Where on earth have you been, Graham? I have been worried sick!'

Martin butted in, 'This is not your son speaking, Mrs Peters. My name is Detective Martin Penn. I am stationed at Hamwell police station.'

'Where?'

'Hamwell, it's in greater London.'

'Oh god, has something happened to my son?'

'Calm down, Mrs Peters. Graham is perfectly safe. He is just helping us with our enquiries.'

'What do you mean, helping you?'

'Graham was arrested at 3.30 a.m. on Wednesday morning and has been held in custody since his arrest.'

'What on earth has he done?'

'You might find this a little hard to believe, Mrs Peters, but it's the truth. When we arrested him, he was down a grave in our local cemetery. He had prised open a one-hundred-year-old coffin and retrieved a sack of gold and silver.'

'No, it must be some mistake.'

'I wish it was, Mrs Peters. Tell me, can you throw any light on this matter?'

'Absolutely none.'

'When we asked him how he knew the gold was in the grave, he said he had dreamt it. Has he been under stress recently?'

'Not to my knowledge, although he did mention once or twice he had a strange dream. I never asked him about it.'

'What does he do for a living?'

'He is a biological scientist. He works with a team of very highly respected scientists trying to find cures for various cancers.'

'This son of yours is a surprise a minute, Mrs Peters. Thank you for your time. One other thing, if you are coming to see him, he could do with a change of clothes. He got quite muddy in that grave.'

'Of course, I will drive up this afternoon.'

'Once again, thank you for your time.'

'No, thank you for informing me. Goodbye.'

Martin was getting more confused by the minute. He sauntered back to where Len was waiting.

'Len, Graham's mother has just told me that her son is a biological scientist, apparently a much-respected one.'

'Why on earth would he jeopardise his career like that, Martin?'

'She also said he had had some strange dreams but couldn't elaborate any further than that.'

'Look, Martin, I know you have your job to do, but could you not postpone officially charging him until after you interview him on Friday? There is a chance you could ruin a very promising career if you act hastily,' Dave butted in. 'Come on, we all know he is as guilty as hell.'

'Shut up, Dave,' Martin snapped. 'I have already decided to do nothing until Friday, and the least we can do is hear him out.' Dave was less than impressed with Martin's decision, venting his anger at the door as he stormed out of the room. Len raised his eyebrows at Martin. 'Somebody is none too happy about your decision.'

'Don't mind him, he can be a little hot-headed at times.'

'I will be off now, Martin. I will see you Friday morning.'

'If I don't get out of here soon, they will have to wheel me home in a barrow,' Martin joked.

The two men left the police station, both of them turning over the day's events, both of them with more questions than answers.

It was late afternoon before Mrs Peters arrived at Hamwell police station. She rang the bell at the front desk, and an officer seemed to appear from nowhere.

'Yes, madam, how can I help you?'

'My name is Mrs Peters. I believe you are holding my son here? I have brought him a clean change of clothes.'

'Mrs Peters, your son is becoming quite the source of speculation in the station.'

'What do you mean?'

'How did he know the gold was in that grave, when to the best of our knowledge, it hasn't been opened since the occupant was buried there over one hundred years ago?'

'I am so pleased he is a source of entertainment for you. Now can you take me to him?'

'He has specifically asked for no visitors until after Friday's interview, Mrs Peters, but if you would like to leave his clothes with me, I will make sure he gets them.'

'No, that's not good enough. I demand to see him.'

'I can understand your anger. I will go down to the cells and see if he is willing to see you.'

The officer disappeared then returned ten minutes later. 'Your son said to thank you for the clothes, and he loves you, but he doesn't want to see anybody until after his statement on Friday.'

The officer noted a little moisture appearing in her eyes. He tactfully turned away, asking if she was staying in town, giving her time to compose herself.

'The George Hotel,' she replied.

'I will make a note of that, and if I get any news, I will phone you. Jot your mobile phone number down on the pad, and don't worry.' She left the station feeling anything but reassured.

CHAPTER FOUR

Thursday morning. Mrs Peters opened the curtains in her room and was greeted by a beautiful sunny day. She pulled up a chair to the window. It didn't take long for her mind to focus on her son's predicament.

'What on earth was he doing? He has always been so level-headed, so methodical in everything he does—it's so out of character.' She was at a complete loss to understand his illogical actions, the rest of the day was spent going over the same questions, and the more she thought about it, the more confused she became.

Len Brown had also been thinking about the case but from a different perspective than Mrs Peters. It was the grave that was occupying his mind. He finished his breakfast and decided to pay the cemetery a visit.

It was late morning before he walked through the cemetery gates. He hadn't been to the cemetery before and strolled around for a while until he found the right grave. Much to Len's surprise, the police had put crime-scene tape around it, and there was a ladder poking out of the top of it. A face appeared at the top of the ladder.

'Hello, Len, what brings you here?'

'Martin, what are you doing, looking for more gold?'

'Very funny. No, I have called in a forensic officer to try and determine if the coffin had been opened before Mr Peters opened it.'

'And had it?'

'I don't know yet. He is still working on it. There is a flask of coffee in my bag. Pour us both a cup and I will join you.'

'What about your colleague?'

'We had better not disturb him. Besides, I've only got two cups.'

'Martin, do you know anything about the occupant of the grave?'

'Nothing whatsoever.'

They both simultaneously turned to the headstone and read the words inscribed on it: 'Annie Philpot, 1862 to 1911, in loving memory of a wonderful wife.'

A man dressed in a pure white overall climbed out of the grave.

'Harry, have you finished?'

'I have Martin.'

'And?'

'And in my expert opinion, the last time the lid was off that coffin was when they placed the occupant inside it.'

'That means', Len deduced, 'that the gold has been lying there for 103 years. If that is true, how on earth did Graham Peters know it was there?'

'That, Len, we will have to wait until tomorrow for the answer.' Martin finished his coffee then offered Harry a cup.

'Thanks, Martin, I could do with a drink.'

The three men stood chatting about peculiar cases they had been involved with.

'A case that I was on about six years ago,' Martin recalled. 'It was not dissimilar to this one in a way.' Martin lit up a cigarette and leaned back, resting himself on a gravestone, and began to tell the story.

'A woman phoned the station saying her neighbours were on holiday and that she could see someone snooping around in their house. We raced to the scene and caught the guy red-handed.' He paused for a moment to drag on his cigarette. Harry was confused.

'What's that got to do with this case?'

'Be patient, and I will tell you. When we asked the burglar how he knew the house owner was on holiday, he said a little bird told him. We kept asking, and he kept replying, "A little bird told me." His luck ran out when we went to search his house. It turned out our man was a pigeon fancier. He had formed a very lucrative partnership with a pigeon-fancying travel agent.'

'I still don't see the connection,' said Harry.

'Well! The plan was when they met up at the quarterly pigeon-fancier's convention, the burglar would leave some of his pigeons with the travel agent, when he had some information for the burglar about people going on holiday he would send it by pigeon, the burglar would settle with the travel agent at every three monthly meetings.'

Harry butted in, 'Is this story going on much longer, Martin? Because I have things to do.'

'No, I am nearly finished. Their luck ran out whilst we were searching the burglar's house. The travel agent decided to send a job through the pigeon post while we were there, so the burglar was telling the truth all along—a little bird did tell him. Do you see the connection? The burglar's excuse was "The little bird told me". Our Mr Peters's excuse is "I dreamt it"—both excuses unbelievable.'

'Yes, I can see that,' said Len.

'I have to go now, Martin, but you will let me know how your man Peters knew the gold was in the grave, won't you?'

'Of course, Harry. And thanks for everything.'

'Before you depart, Harry—'

'Yes, Len?'

'Did you hear the one about the farmer who rang the police station saying "Somebody has poisoned my chicken feed and I have now got four chickens that are ill"?'

The officer who answered the phone replied, 'Don't worry, sir, I will send out a forensic officer.'

'Is that it?' said Martin. Both he and Harry stood blank faced, expecting more to come. 'Don't you get it? Do I have to explain it? The officer said he would send out a four-hens-sick officer.'

'That one sounds like it came out of a cracker,' Martin jibed.

Harry, however, was breaking his sides with laughter. 'I must remember that one to tell them back at the forensic laboratory.'

The three men said their good-byes and went their separate ways.

As Martin reported for duty on Thursday evening Jack called him over. 'Dave has phoned in. He won't be in tonight, and he said he has been feeling sick all day.'

'Shit! I was hoping for a quiet night. I wanted to get my head down for a couple of hours. I have an interview in the morning.'

'Would that be with Peter's?'

'That's right, the dreamer.'

'There is quite a bit of interest in the station as to how he knew the gold was in the grave, and that includes me.'

'Well, Jack! Tomorrow, hopefully all will be revealed.'

'It should be a quiet night, Martin, it's not like it's the weekend, and I will only call you if something urgent crops up.'

'I appreciate that, Jack, see you later.' He could rely on Jack, a 1950s Jamaican immigrant, who still kept his West Indian accent, a deep baritone voice, and a person who you could trust your life with.

Martin's luck held out; not a punch-up, a robbery, or a domestic came in all night. Early Friday morning, Martin spent time trying to find someone to support him in the interview room. Although Dave had let him down, it didn't seem to bother him much. If anything, he was quite relieved, he could now conduct the interview at his own pace.

Sergeant Ernie Edwards was busy sorting where to deploy his PCs for the day, Martin pulled him to one side. 'Ernie.'

'Hello, Martin, what can I do for you?' Martin and Ernie went back a long way, they both joined the force at about the same time, and Martin was best man at Ernie's wedding.

'I need someone to sit in with me at an interview this morning. Dave Harris has phoned in sick. I wondered if you could spare one of your PCs.'

'I do believe I have just the person—WPC Pam Turner, she's keen, intelligent, and quite a looker.'

'Perfect! Thanks, Ernie, will you send her along to the interview room when she's ready?'

'No problem.' Martin made his way to the interview room to run through his notes.

Len had his usual light breakfast—muesli and a coffee. Although in his late thirties, he could still make the ladies give him a second glance. He also had a roving eye for the fairer sex; he never liked to leave home in the morning anything less than impeccably dressed. Before setting off, he went through his regular routine of standing in front of the full-length mirror, eyeing himself up and down, checking his tailor-made pinstripe suit was free of loose hairs and dandruff. With a white shirt and red tie and a sharp crease in his trousers and shiny black shoes, he was now ready for the world to enjoy the wonder of Len. He picked up his briefcase and made his way to the police station.

Arriving at the police station at 9.45 a.m., he signed in and made straight for the canteen to snatch a quick coffee. Martin was also in the canteen. He was sitting opposite Pam Turner, hurriedly bringing her up-to-date with the events so far. On conclusion of the briefing, they both rose from their chairs and made their way to the interview room. Martin noticed Len drinking his coffee.

Walking up behind him, he tapped his shoulder and quietly said, 'Ready when you are, Len.'

Graham Peters had finished his breakfast. He had to admit to himself that the food was a darn sight better than he had expected. He was now sitting in the interview room, with a burly officer standing guard behind him. The door opened. Martin, Pam, and Len entered. Martin spoke first. 'Thanks Officer. You can return to your duties now.'

Len sat down next to Graham. 'Have you had breakfast yet, Graham?' he enquired.

'Yes, thank you, Len. I must say I am quite impressed with the way I have been treated so far.'

'Good. If you need my advice, remember I am right here for you.'

Martin and Pam took the seats opposite. 'You haven't been introduced yet, have you, Len? Pam, this is Peter's brief, Len Brown, and Len, this is WPC Pamela Turner.'

'Hello, Len.'

'Pamela.'

If there was one thing that got Len's sexual fantasies working overtime, it was the sight of a young blond WPC in a tight-fitting uniform. How disappointed he would be if he knew what Pam was thinking. She was studying the young man sitting next to him. She was thinking, *What a polite young man and so good-looking.* His hair was dark brown, almost black, as were his eyebrows. Although he had shaved that morning, he still sported very definite stubble, which Pam found extremely attractive in a man. His eyes were blue—*kind eyes*, she thought—but they showed signs of torment. His voice told her that he was educated but not posh. *What on earth drove him to the point where he ended up in the situation he now finds himself in?* she wondered.

Martin switched on the tape recorder. 'Interviewing Graham Peters on the desecration of a grave and possession of a substantial

19

amount of gold and silver. People present myself, DI Martin Penn, WPC Pamela Turner, Graham Peters, and his solicitor, Leonard Brown.' He turned to Graham. 'Well, Mr Peters, you said you wanted to explain yourself. Well, this is your moment.'

Graham took a deep breath. 'You might remember me saying earlier this week that my story seemed so implausible that I could hardly believe it. First I will ask you a question. Do you believe in life after death?'

Martin leaned back in his chair. 'With all due respect, Mr Peters, how much longer must we listen to this clap trap?'

Len came straight back in Graham's defence. 'Give him a chance, Martin. He has hardly opened his mouth yet.'

'Sorry! You're absolutely right. Carry on, Mr Peters.'

'Like I was saying, could it be just possible that there is a way that someone who is dead can communicate with the living? I am not talking about zombies walking around but something much more plausible, because I believe that is what is happening to me. For example, a person can pass on their characteristics to their next of kin. How many times have you heard somebody say "He is his father's double" or "Hasn't she got her mother's eyes?" So on that same principle, is it not possible that one's thoughts can be passed from generation to generation then in a future moment in time, those inherited thoughts reawaken in the form of dreams? When a cuckoo chick hatches, the first thing it does is to toss all the other eggs out of the nest. It has had no training from the parent bird, so the most logical explanation is the DNA knowledge has been passed on from parent to chick. Take the turtle, for another example. It comes ashore and digs a hole in the sand, lays its eggs, and buries them. The young hatch and instinctively know that after being born in complete darkness under the ground, they must climb to the surface and scamper down to the beach as fast as possible. I know I am beginning to ramble on a bit, but I will give you one more example. Salmon—they are born in a freshwater river and instinctively know that at a certain time in their development, they must swim hundreds of miles out to sea to live in a saltwater environment.'

Pam was already captivated by this young man's logic and confidence. She couldn't wait for him to continue.

'What I am saying is, can the DNA, the building blocks of life, store information that can resurface in later generations?'

'An interesting theory, Mr Peters, but—and it's a *big* but—can you prove it?' Martin questioned.

'Yes, I believe I can, to a 99 per cent proof of probability.'

'I, for one, will be very interested to hear how you intend to convince us,' Martin scoffed.

'You may or may not be aware that my profession is a biological scientist. Believe me, I am not bragging when saying that. It's just that in a way, it's not dissimilar to your job, Officer. We both need to have method, order, and a questioning mind.'

Martin nodded in agreement.

Graham continued, 'It all started quite innocently about six months ago. I had gone to bed at my usual time, about 11.30 p.m. I hadn't overeaten or watched a horrific film, so there were no aggravating factors to make me dream such a vivid dream. I dreamt I was being chased down a street. I was scared. People were shouting. There was a wall. I climbed over it. I was now hiding in an undertaker's back room surrounded by coffins. All were empty bar one—there was a woman laid out in it. I hid there for a while then made my way home, where a woman was waiting angrily for me. "Arthur Tidwell! What time do you call this?" she screeched. I awoke sweating profusely. I mentioned it to my mother in the morning, but she was busy getting ready for work and said that I should lay off eating cheese in the evening.'

'At least that tallies with what your mother told me,' stated Martin, as if that was the first piece of common sense that had surfaced from this so-called interview. Len was feeling redundant but was really enjoying this oddest of interviews. Pam was loving it. Graham could talk all day long as far as she was concerned.

'The dreams continued, not always exactly the same, but the fear was always present. The coffin featured a lot in them. Even the occupant had a name—Annie Philpot.'

'That would be the person in the grave that you thoughtlessly dug up?' said Martin, not letting Graham get too cosy with his story.

'I wish there were another way to prove my theory, but there isn't.'

Len interrupted. 'The question we all want to know, Graham, is how did you know the gold and silver was in that grave?'

'That's it—I didn't. I guessed it was there, based on the evidence that I had gathered from where my dreams had led me. Incidentally, Officer, when I have finished my story, I hope you will agree with me that I have solved a 103-year-old robbery and murder.'

'In that case, please continue,' Martin said rather sarcastically.

Graham was beginning to enjoy himself. He could finally tell someone the whole story. His confidence was building. He could see the young lady sitting opposite was already spellbound by his story, and he could sense just a little more interest being shown by the two Doubting Thomases.

'My dreams continued nightly, and I was beginning to think there was something wrong with me. Yet another name kept cropping up—Goldstein. Where were these names coming from? Were they real people? To the best of my knowledge, I didn't know anybody with these names. At one stage, I seriously thought of visiting a shrink. My dreams continued, and they do even to this very day.'

Martin interrupted again. 'Would anybody like a cup of coffee?'

Pam and Len both welcomed the suggestion. Martin noticed Graham didn't answer. 'That does include you, Mr Peters.'

'Thank you. I would love one.'

Martin left the room for a moment then returned, saying, 'The coffees are on their way.'

Graham continued, 'May tenth this year was my granny's birthday. Mum asked me if I would like to accompany her to see Gran. At first I declined the invitation. "Oh, please come?" she said. "The change of scenery will do you good, and you know how pleased she always is to see you." I couldn't argue with her logic, so I gave in to her request.'

A knock on the door interrupted the proceedings. A short, overweight lady gingerly opened the door, holding a tray of coffee and biscuits.

Martin spoke. 'Just leave it on the table, Mrs Thomas. We will take it from here.'

Pam played mother and distributed the coffees and biscuits.

Graham thanked her and continued his story. 'Although my gran is in her seventies and a little wobbly on her feet, her mind is still as sharp as a razor. She noticed I was looking a little gaunt and asked me if everything was all right. I replied I hadn't been sleeping too well and was having some strange dreams. Mum said I should get myself a girlfriend.'

Pam butted in, 'Have you got one yet?'

'No, but I am still looking,' Graham replied.

Pam had already been ticking the boxes for Graham as a potential boyfriend, and that last answer ticked a very big box indeed.

'Anyway,' he continued, 'she asked me about my dreams. I told her of the fear and the names that kept surfacing every night.

'"What names are they, Graham?" she said. "Well, three names came up regularly—Annie Philpot, Goldstein, and Arthur Tidwell," I replied.

'"Did you say Arthur Tidwell? Why, that was the name of my grandfather."

'"You're kidding me, Gran," I said. I was flabbergasted.

"'No, Graham, it was Arthur Tidwell."

'I asked her about the other two names, but she had never heard of them. "Can you tell me anything about him, Gran?" was my next question.

"'Actually I can, Graham," she said as though she had something juicy to divulge. "According to my gran, he was a bit of a bad lot."

"'In what way?" I asked.

"'His wife, my gran, told me that she had suspected that he had done something really bad. Even though he never confided in her, she knew it lay heavy on his mind. Whatever it was stayed a secret because he took it to his grave with him. He left her with a nine-month-old baby to bring up. She never forgave him for that."

"'Would that child have been your mother?" I asked.

"'That is correct," she replied.

'She had sparked my interest. I wanted to know more. "What year did he die?" I asked.

"'I think it was 1913. Yes, that's right—1913. He committed suicide, you know. It got into the local paper. He also left a suicide note. I still have it somewhere," she said.

'I asked if I could see it.

"'Of course you can," she said. "It's in an old box in the cupboard under the stairs with the rest of Gran's effects."

'My next question was, "Whereabouts did he live?"

"'Not around here. Somewhere in London. Hamwell, I think the name was."

'I went to the cupboard. It was packed solid with junk, and she even had my mother's old pushchair in there. I joked to her, "Mum, I bet you can't still fit in here." She laughed, saying something about fitting me in it if I didn't behave myself. I eventually found a battered old box with the words *Sunlight Soap* written on the side. I lifted it out and emptied the contents on to a table. There amongst a few pieces of memorabilia was a folded-up piece of paper. I opened it carefully and started to read. It was plainly obvious that the writer was a person of little to no education—the grammar and spelling was awful. It started by telling his wife of his shame and guilt at something he had done. He never mentioned what it was. Then his goodbyes—he ended by wishing his wife and his nine-month-old daughter a happy life.

'Mother and I spent the rest of the afternoon with Gran, and we set off for home after tea. The drive home was about forty miles. I am afraid I wasn't the best of driving companions on the journey home. My mind was working overtime, trying to analyse the day's revelations. I don't know why, but I felt I needed to know more about this ancient relative of mine. I had two weeks' holiday due to me, so I decided to take them the following week. What I had intended to do was to come here to Hamwell and see what if anything I could learn about Arthur Tidwell. I didn't tell Mum exactly where I was going or why I was going there. Perhaps I felt a little embarrassed. I told her I was going to London for a change of scenery. She thought I was going to see the sights. It was the twenty-seventh of June when I arrived in Hamwell. I booked in at the Ferryman Hotel on Bridge Street, and I don't know if any of you know it, but it's a charming little hotel with so much history.'

Len had visited it many times but not for its historic value. He always had somebody else's wife or girlfriend to accompany him, and one night was the maximum duration of his visits.

'My god!' said Martin. 'It's one p.m. The canteen closes at two p.m. Let's stop for some lunch and resume at 1.45 p.m. I think it will be okay for you to dine with us, Peters. I don't think you're a risk to society.'

All four made their way to the canteen with Martin leading the way. The menu was a little lacking in choice—fish and chips, steak and kidney pie, jacket potato with various fillings, or salad. Martin recommended the pie to Graham, adding he would have it put on his tag, knowing Graham was not carrying any money. Pam chose the jacket potato with a tuna filling and Len the salad, always conscious of his figure.

The tables sat two people only. Graham sat down first, and Pam joined him. 'This story of yours,' she said, 'it's fascinating. I can't wait to hear more.'

'Thanks,' he said. 'Do you mind if I call you Pam?' He didn't like to call her *miss* or *Constable*; it just didn't seem right somehow.

'Of course not, but not in the interview room.' She was saying it wouldn't be right for the accused and the accuser to be on first-name terms.

Len and Martin were discussing the possibility that Graham was telling the truth.

'He bloody well better be or I will throw the book at him,' said Martin.

'What you can do', suggested Len, 'is make a call to the Ferryman Hotel and see if they have a booking for a Graham Peters on June 27.'

After they had all finished lunch, Martin suggested that if anyone wanted to go to the toilet, they should go now before they went back. All four went. On their return, Martin instructed Pam to escort Graham and Len back to the interview room, adding he had something important to do. He returned to his office, immediately picked up the phone, dialled a number, then spoke. 'The Ferryman Hotel please, Bridge Street, Hamwell.'

The voice at the other end said, 'Connecting you now, sir.' A couple of seconds later, a woman's voice spoke. 'Ferryman Hotel, Polly speaking, how may I help you?'

Martin introduced himself. 'I am making inquiries regarding a Mr Graham Peters. Can you tell me if he stayed with you for any period of time from the twenty-seventh of June to mid-July this year?'

'It will take a minute or two. Please hold the line.'

He heard the sound of the receiver being placed on the reception desk, followed by the flipping over of pages. It seemed no more than a few seconds before she lifted the receiver again. 'Mr Peters booked one week's stay with us commencing on the twenty-seventh of June. He extended his stay for another five days. He finally checked out on July 9.' Martin thanked her for her help then headed back to the interview room. He didn't mention where he had been or what he was doing. He just pulled up his seat saying, 'Okay, Peters, continue.'

'I had no idea what I was looking for or why or what on earth I expected to find. Where do I start? I asked myself. I decided my first port of call would be the local cemetery. I rang for a taxi to take me there as I had no idea where it was, on arrival I thought I might try and find the grave of my ancestor, Arthur Tidwell. I methodically read every gravestone,'

'Did you find it?' said Pam, eager to hear more.

'There were a couple that could have been his, but they were in such a state of disrepair it was hard to tell. However one of the gravestones read "Annie Philpot, 1862 to 1911. In loving memory of a wonderful wife". This was one of the names that appeared in my dreams. I sat on a small headstone for a moment, trying to analyse the connection between my dreams and these people whom I knew really existed. How did they manage to get into my dreams? Did my relative have an affair with Annie? Or even scarier, did Arthur Tidwell murder Annie Philpot?'

Len asked, 'Why did you think that, Graham?'

'Well, I looked at my dream evidence. First a troubled man who was frightened and ridden with shame and guilt, enough to make him commit suicide, and an image of a woman in my dreams stretched out in a coffin, and the dates that they both died—Annie, 1911, and Arthur, two years later. I thought it was quite a reasonable assumption. If Arthur had killed Annie, then it seemed reasonable to assume that the fear and guilt that built up in him over the next two years became too much for him to bear, thus resulting in him taking his own life, but where did the name *Goldstein* come in my dreams?

'Tell me, have any of you ever been somewhere that you were absolutely certain you had never been to before but had the strangest of feelings that you had?'

Martin, much to Graham's surprise, said, 'Yes, I have.' No sooner had he opened his big mouth than he wished he had banged himself over the head with his truncheon. But he wasn't getting away with that scot free.

'Well, come on, sir. Don't leave it at that,' said Pam.

Len also pressed him to tell all.

He gave them both a look that could have easily turned them both into stone, then reluctantly agreed to tell of his experience. 'My wife and I originate from Yorkshire. Neither of us had ever visited London before. The Met was advertising for recruits from within the force, so I spoke to my wife asking her if she fancied the idea of living in London. She jumped at the idea, and so I applied for the position of detective and, to my amazement, was accepted. We both took a week's holiday to come down to London to go house-hunting.'

'How exciting. I would love to go house-hunting,' said Pam, glancing in Graham's direction.

'Believe me when I say it's not as pleasurable as you might imagine. We viewed numerous properties—none of them had that "come and live in me" feeling. We eventually came to the house we live in now. As soon as I opened the front door, it felt familiar. I seemed to know the layout of every room even though I had never set foot in the house before. To cut a long story short, we put a deposit down on it and moved in two months later. Like all women, the first thing my wife wanted to do was decorate. We started with the master bedroom. Now here is the strange thing that I have never been able to find a logical explanation for. When I began to strip the wallpaper off, written on the bare wall behind were the words, "Hello, Martin". It quite unnerved me for a while, but with the new job and the decorating, I didn't have time to dwell on it.'

'That is a shame,' said Graham. 'There might have been an explanation that could have given you answers if you searched a little deeper.'

'That may be so, Mr Peters, but we are not here to listen to what I have to say. So if you don't mind, please continue.'

'You are right, Officer. As you have just heard, we all have those unexplained feelings. Most of the time, we can shrug them off as a coincidence. However, my feelings had what I would call substance to back them up. The next day, I was in two minds where to continue my investigation. The cemetery had no more secrets to give up. I thought I might take a walk around the town. The weather forecast ruled out rain, so I opted for walking there. I strolled down the High Street, looking both left and right for any insignificant little clue to continue my quest, but alas, I drew a complete blank. At the top end of the High street, I turned right into Broad Street. It was there that I started to get feelings of déjà vu. In contrast to the more modern buildings of the High Street, Broad Street looked a lot less affected by progress, with Tudor-style buildings still standing proudly amongst some more recently built ones. There is a small alleyway halfway along the street. I don't know if any of you know it—blink and you will miss it—it's called the Mews. For some reason, my interest was drawn to this little alleyway. A few yards along the cobbled road on one side, there is an old wall about five feet high. I climbed up and peered over. There is a courtyard approximately twelve yards square. It has three small outhouses surrounding it. They are all in rundown condition. It was obvious they had not seen any useful employ for many a year. Somehow I thought this place was important to me but I couldn't think why. Walking back to Broad Street, I noticed the front of the building read "Smithers and Son, Solicitors Established Since 1925".

Plucking up courage, I went inside. A rather attractive receptionist sat behind a desk, manicuring her fingernails.

"'Good afternoon, sir. How can I help you?"

'The words rolled off her tongue as if she had said them a thousand times before. I made up a story that I was researching the history of Broad Street and asked if she could tell me if the solicitors were the first business to occupy the building. She said she didn't know, saying she hadn't been around then. I joked, "If you were, you have worn exceptionally well, and can you give me the name of your face cream?" I thought my little quip was amusing—however, she ignored it and carried on.

"'Let me phone through to Mr Smithers," she said. "If anybody would know, he will." She phoned through to her boss. "I have a young man here in reception. He is researching the history of Broad Street, and could you spare him a moment of your time? You are in luck," she said. "Mr Smithers said he can give you five minutes. It's the first floor, second door on the right."

'The creaking of the stairs gave one a good insight to the age of the building. It was very Victorian in its looks, with a fusty smell that was ingrained in the whole building. Mr Smithers's room, however, was very different again. It was really twenty-first century with every modern office appliance known to man. I introduced myself, then he pointed to a chair and beckoned me to sit down. I said I was from the local gazette and was researching the history of Broad Street.

"'How very interesting," he said, "but how can I help?"

"'No disrespects, sir," I said, "but I would imagine this building has been on Broad Street since day one. Has Smithers and Son occupied the building from the beginning?"

"'Good heavens, no," he chuckled. "My father took over the lease in 1925. It had been vacant for one year. Before that, it was a cobbler's—that's a shoemaker to you young folk."

'"I didn't know that," I said, not wanting to stop his outpouring of information. "Do you know how long the shoe shop traded here?" I asked.

'"About ten years," he said.

'Working it out in my brain, that took us back to 1914. It was the period before then that I was most interested in. "I would really like to be able to go back to the turn of the century. Do you know who had it then?" I asked.

'He thought long and hard then shrugged his shoulders. "No, sorry, I can't help you there," he said apologetically.

'"Thank you for your time, Mr Smithers," I said, feeling a tad deflated. I arose from my chair and shook his hand then turned to leave. I was just about to close the door behind me when he called me back. "Hold on a moment, young man. I remember my father telling me it was an undertaker's."

'"Thank you, sir," I said. "Thank you very much." That is what I half expected to hear, but nevertheless, I was still mildly surprised when he said it. My dreams and the reality of my investigations seemed to be so closely related that the possibility that there was no link between them was becoming much less likely.'

Martin, Len, and Pam sat spellbound, listening to Graham's account of events. What Martin once thought was a lot of claptrap was now making a lot of sense to him.

Pam spoke. 'What about Goldstein? Did you ever find out who he or she was?' She was itching to know the answer.

'Yes, I did,' he continued. 'I wanted to find somewhere to sit quietly and digest my new information. There is a little inn down Broad Street. Its name is the Long Boat. Feeling a little thirsty, I went inside, ordered a pint and a ploughman's, and found a quiet corner to eat and think. A theory was forming in my mind. Were my dreams telling me about something that happened to someone else over a hundred years ago? If so, why was it happening to me, and who the heck was Goldstein? Unbeknown to me, the answer was literally staring me in the face. I finished my meal and made my way to the front door. All along the wall, there were photographs of Broad Street stretching way back from since the invention of the camera. One thing I really like doing is looking over old historic photos, and so I browsed over them on the way out. Can you imagine my amazement when there, in front of me, was a photo of a row of shops, and the sign above one of the shops read "H. Goldstein Jewellers and Goldsmith"? I was so excited that I returned to the inn, ordered another coffee, and sat down on the same seat that I had just risen from. It was time to put all my knowledge up for scrutiny.'

CHAPTER FIVE

Tongues were beginning to get a little dry, and bottoms, fidgety. Len interrupted the proceedings. 'Martin, is there any chance of a drink?' Pam said she was also parched, Martin agreed to the request and instructed Pam to order the coffees 'Let's pause a moment to stretch our legs until she returns,' suggested Martin. All three men began to stride around the interview room, stretching their legs, bending their backs, and rubbing their backsides. Pam returned; she stood in the doorway.

'Oh my god! You have turned it into a fitness club,' she laughed.

'OK, Constable, we get it. Now let's get back to our seats,' said Martin, who by now had given up any attempt at an interview and, like the other two, just wanted to hear the end of the story.

Graham continued. 'Now where was I? Oh yes! I was—and still am—having vivid dreams nightly. I strongly believe that they are in some way connected to a distant relative of mine. The reasoning behind my logic was based on what my grandmother had told me—that he was a bad lot. I also know he was a troubled soul—that is what her grandmother told her. Where Annie Philpot fitted in was still a mystery. I knew she died two years before my relative, and she appeared in my dreams in a coffin, and also, she was buried in your local cemetery and just possibly laid out in one of outbuildings behind Smithers and Son.'

'You would make a good detective, Peters,' joked Martin.

'Thanks, but no thanks,' Graham replied. 'This investigation has nearly sent me to the funny farm.' Graham took a sip of coffee then continued.

'Goldstein, where on earth did that name fit into this puzzle? All I knew about the name was it appeared in my dreams and there was a goldsmith with the same name. My next move was to look through a telephone directory for anybody with the name Goldstein. There were four Goldsteins in the book, and I phoned them all. The question I asked was, "There used to be a jeweller's and goldsmith in Broad Street with the name of Goldstein, and could you tell me if they were a distant relative of yours? After drawing a blank with three of them, I finally struck lucky. A man's voice answered.'

'"Yes," he said, "he was my great-great grandfather."

'"That's fantastic," I said. "My name is Graham Peters, and I am researching the history of Broad Street, and there seems to be no information available regarding your relative's shop,' I told him where I was staying and that if he fancied a free dinner, we could arrange a time to meet. I could hear a woman's voice in the background shouting at him, "Jeff, will you get off of that phone? The twins' nappies need changing. Have I got to do everything?" she screamed.

'Jeff whispered down the phone at me, "Look, mate, I can't speak now, but I will see you tomorrow at one p.m. at the Ferryman."

'I started to thank him for his time, but he was gone—nappy changing, I would imagine.'

'The next morning I spent in the bar wondering what information Jeffrey Goldstein could give me, if any. At about 1.05 p.m., a young man in jeans and trainers walked into the bar. He was very slim, almost to the point of being undernourished. He looked most ill at ease, as if he were not used to visiting upper-class establishments such as the Ferryman. I walked up to him, saying, "Excuse me, but is your name Jeff?"

"'Yes," he said. "But how did you know?" He looked at me with suspicion.

"'My name is Graham," I said, "and I heard your wife screaming your name to come and change the twin's nappies when I phoned you."

'I think I might have embarrassed him because his face went bright red. "Shall we sit down? What would you like to drink?" I said. He asked for a pint, and I had the same. We sat down, and I showed him the food menu. I said that I would be having the sirloin and for him to order whatever he wished. He looked at the menu and gasped, "Are these prices for real?" Nevertheless, he still ordered a T-bone steak and attacked it like a vulture. I waited until he finished before I broached the subject of his great-great-grandfather.

'Jeff said, "When he was alive, I have been told our family was quite well off, but the family fortunes changed overnight."

"'Why is that?" I asked.

"'One fateful night in November in the year 1911, my great-great-grandfather was working late in his shop when somebody broke in. He couldn't have known my great-great-granddad was still there. A fight took place. Great-great-granddad received a fatal blow on the head. The assailant cleared the shop of every valuable there was in the shop. Two policemen were passing by and gave chase. It was a foggy night. They chased him halfway down Broad Street, but he managed to give them the slip. That left my great-great-grandma destitute. The family has never really bounced back to good fortune again. The items that he stole never ever turned up. Sometimes I wonder, if my great- great-granddad hadn't decided to work late that night, how different our lives would be now.

'After he had finished his story, I have to admit that I felt awful. I was 99 per cent sure that Arthur Tidwell, my distant relative, was the one responsible for the Goldsteins' pain and misfortune. My heart really went out to Jeff. He was obviously finding life tough trying to provide for a wife and twins. When we parted company, I offered him £20 to buy his twins a little treat. He refused it at first, but I forced it in his hand. Somehow I felt responsible for his family's situation.

'"Thanks," he said then invited me to come home with him to see his little bundles of joy. I thanked him for his kind invitation but declined it, making the excuse that I still had a lot more research to do but asked him to leave me his address and said that I would try and get round to see them later in the week. I could see the disappointment register in his face.

'After he had left, I felt awful. I thought to myself, *You swine, Peters. Hasn't your family heaped enough misery on the Goldsteins?* My guilt got the better of me, and two days later, I found myself knocking on their door. His wife answered the door. I don't know why, but I was expecting a taller woman than the one standing before me. Perhaps it was the image I conjured up of her after listening to her ranting on the phone. She actually seemed rather pleasant. I introduced myself, "My name is Graham," but before I could utter another word, she said, "You're Jeff's friend, please come in."

'Jeff's friend? I thought, *I wouldn't exactly go that far.* But nevertheless, I went along with it. She led me into the lounge where Jeff was sitting, bouncing the twins up and down on his knees, saying, "Gee-gee ride." Their chuckling little laughs were quite infectious. He placed the twins on the settee, stood up, and greeted me with far more warmth than necessary or, to my shame, that I deserved, although I did have the forethought to pop into the shops before my visit. I bought the twins a cuddly teddy bear each and a box of chocolates for his wife, Mary. I don't think she received

many treats because she couldn't stop thanking me, and Jeff kept pushing the teddy bear in the twins' face saying, "Look, James. Look, Jeffrey, it's a teddy bear." Little James and Jeffrey were just beginning to walk, and their father got them to waddle across to where I was sitting and say thank you to me. They came waddling over and in their cute little voices said, "Fan–q." I found them a refreshingly loving family who deserved a change of fortune.'

Len butted in, 'Can I interrupt you there, Graham?' Directing his question across the table to Martin, he asked, 'How long do the police keep the records of unsolved murders?'

'Quite a long time, but if you are thinking what I think you are thinking, I very much doubt if it is that long,' said Martin.

Len suggested there would be no harm in checking. Martin turned to Pam. 'Go and see if you can find someone in charge of records, and ask them if there is a remote chance they have anything relating to the murder of a Mr Goldstein in the year 1911. Try and find Alan Palmer. If anyone knows, he will.'

Pam was less than pleased to be dragged away from Graham's story, but she need not have worried though because Martin who had been gasping for a cigarette decided to use this opportunity to call a ten-minute break. He slipped out the back and lit up, leaving Len and Graham to talk to each other. 'I can honestly say, Graham, I have never sat in an interview that is so interesting and so implausible, and yet so believable.'

'I can assure you, Len, every word I have spoken is the absolute truth.'

'Let's hope they find something in their records to support your story.'

'Surely,' Graham said. 'They wouldn't keep records that long.'

No sooner had Martin returned, smelling like an ashtray, than Pam burst in, waving a folder. She stood in the doorway and made a victorious pose, saying, 'Guess what I've got?'

Len just said, 'Bloody marvellous.'

Martin uttered, not once but twice, 'I don't believe it. I just don't bloody believe it.'

Graham couldn't wait to hear the contents of the report and made the mistake of calling her Pam when asking her to bring it over. Fortunately, no one picked up on his little slip of the tongue.

Martin took charge of the report. It was a brown cardboard sleeve, rolled up and tied with string. He took a penknife out of his pocket, cut the string, and opened the folder and started to read to himself. Almost immediately, a chorus of protests greeted him. 'Read it out aloud, Martin. We all want to hear it.'

'OK, it starts with a Sergeant John Blake giving his account of the night of the murder and robbery. This is what he wrote.

'On the night of 9 November 1911, at 7.30 p.m., I and Constable Tom Price were patrolling the back of the shops in Broad Street. While passing the jewellers known as H. Goldstein, we noticed the back gate was open and a light was shining inside. We both went in to inform Mr Goldstein that he had left his back gate open, when a man holding a sack barged past us, knocking Tom over. We gave chase; he ran into Broad Street. It was a foggy night, and he gave us the slip. We searched the area for approximately half an hour, but he was long gone. We then returned to the jeweller's and found Mr Goldstein lying on the floor of his shop. He had a head wound and was unconscious. We called for a doctor who confirmed at the scene of the crime that Mr Goldstein had died of his injury. That is about all there is really. It does go on about who he reported it to and so on, so, Mr Peters, it appears your story does have an element of truth to it.'

'Thank you, Officer. I have been trying to tell you that all day.'

Pam, who by now had absolutely no doubt Graham was telling the truth, the whole truth, and nothing but the truth, then asked him what he did after he left Jeff's house.

'Well, Pam, I mean Constable,'—Pam blushed—'I think I must have made quite an impression because they all came to the front door and waved me off. I think I made a particular impression on Mary, because she hugged me and gave me a peck on the cheek saying "Do come and see us soon." I said I would, but I left with a heavy heart, knowing I had lied my way into their lives. My holiday was coming to an end, and so I returned to the Ferryman Hotel and started to pack. I had learned a lot from my visit to Hamwell, but work called, so I checked out on July 9 and made my way back to Portsmouth. Incidentally, I left my car in a cul-de-sac close to the cemetery in Spring Close. If you are going to return me into custody, could I ask you to collect it and leave it in the police station car park until you release me?'

Martin laughed. 'I don't think I have met anyone so laid-back about being locked up. But don't worry, I don't think you will be spending another night in jail—that is, unless we find out it was you who killed Mr Goldstein in 1911.'

'My client definitely pleads not guilty to that one,' said Len, continuing the humour.

'That's good,' Graham sighed. 'Shall I continue?'

'Please do,' said Martin.

'The following Monday, I returned back to work. I found it very hard to settle into the old routine, and it wasn't long before my team leader, Professor Irvin, noticed that my mind was not on my work. One morning he called me into his office.

'"Look, Graham," he said. "It hasn't gone unnoticed that since your return from holiday, you haven't been yourself. It is affecting your work, and you know that we are a small unit here and we can't afford passengers. Any wrong conclusions you arrive at in your work could set the whole team back months, if not years. If you have a problem, let me hear it now. I really don't want to have to make you step down from our work. You show great promise, and I would hate to lose you."

'I saw no point in trying to deny his claims. He was absolutely right—I wasn't focused on my work.

'We spent all morning discussing my problem in his office. I told him about my dreams, my chance remark to my gran, who had connected my dreams to Arthur Tidwell, my great-great-grandfather; the suicide note my gran kept in the sunlight soap box; my visit to Hamwell cemetery where I discovered the second person in my dreams; Annie Philpot; the feeling of déjà vu. Whilst walking down Broad Street, Smithers and Son and how it was once an undertaker's The discovery of Goldstein's shop in the photograph on the wall of the Long Boat, Jeff and Mary Goldstein, and Jeff's story about his great-great grandfather that had been handed down from past generations, and how the dreams continued even to this very day.

'Professor Irvin thought for a while. He is a wonderful scientist with a brilliant mind. Surprisingly he never dismissed my story as—how did you call it, Officer?—"a load of clap trap". Instead he asked me if I had any theories of what was happening to me. I said it seemed to me that someone was trying to contact me from the grave, a kind of inherited thought.

'"That, Graham, is a very interesting theory. Do you have any idea who it might be?" he asked.

'"If it is anyone, it is my great-great grandfather."

'"Why do you think it was him?" he questioned.

'"I know this sounds a little crazy, but I think he wants me to right a great wrong. I think he robbed and murdered Mr Goldstein. I also think he wants me to find the loot and return it to the Goldstein family."

'"And do you know where the loot is?"

'"No, I haven't got a clue."

'"As strange as this may seem, Graham," he said, "I think your theory has a lot going for it. What I want you to do is take some time off to sort your problem out. You are not a lot of good to the team in your present state of mind. I will make up some excuse to tell the team. I will say I have sent you on a course."

'I thanked him for listening to my story and for his understanding. I can't tell you how much it meant to me that somebody had listened to me without thinking I had just escaped from the funny farm.

'"Now you go and attack your problem with the same professionalism and method that you have shown here. Maybe Annie Philpot hasn't given up all her secrets yet."

'*What a strange thing to say*, I thought, then I left.'

CHAPTER SIX

'For two weeks I grappled with my problem, going through the events of the past without any sign of a breakthrough. My dreams still featured a troubled Arthur Tidwell and Annie Philpot laying prostrate in her coffin, and on the odd occasion Goldstein would pop in for a visit, I started to think about what Professor Irvin's last words were. Annie Philpot might have more secrets to surrender, and then it hit me—if Arthur had been greeted by his screaming wife and he never had the loot with him, what would he have done with it? Of course he would have hidden it. And where would he hide it? In Annie's coffin. And the reason he never collected it was either he had found out that he had killed Goldstein or Annie had been buried before he had the chance to retrieve it.

"That is it!" I shouted out aloud to myself. "Thank you, Professor." The more I thought about it, the more convinced I was becoming that I had solved the puzzle. The question now was what to do about it.'

Graham was on a roll and was not going to stop until his audience had heard every little snippet of his story. 'My first thoughts were of Jeff, Mary, and their twin boys, little Jeffrey and James. After all, it was their family that had suffered the most from my family's crime. Yes, I thought I would return it to the Goldstein family—that would be the fitting thing to do, and it would go a long way in righting the wrong that Arthur Tidwell had inflicted on Jeff's family, and also, it would ease my conscience by a considerable degree. If I went to Hamwell cemetery and dug up Annie's grave in the middle of the night, retrieved the loot, then filled in the grave again, no one would ever know. It was not like anybody had been lovingly attending it. I pooh-poohed that idea as too risky. My second thought was to go to Portsmouth police station and ask to speak to a detective for advice. I made my mind up that this was the more responsible action to take, so one morning, that is what I decided to do. When I entered the police station, I asked the man at the reception desk if it was possible to speak to a detective.'

"'What about?" he said.

"'A robbery and murder," I replied. That seemed to focus his interest a little more. He asked me to take a seat while he phoned upstairs for a detective. Like a good boy, I did exactly what I was told. I sat and I sat, and I sat for the best part of an hour before I was finally seen. A giant of a detective marched up to me. He had the tact and discretion of a gorilla.

"'My name is Detective William Sykes," he said. "Are you the guy who wants to report a murder?"

"'Yes," I replied.

"'Well, let's hear it then. Spit it out."

"'Shouldn't we go somewhere a little more private?" I said, feeling a little embarrassed at telling my story while people were walking by all the time.

"'No, if you have something to say, you can say it right here."

'*Do put a man at ease*, I thought. *After all, I am only going to solve a murder for you, you big baboon.* I was now feeling really nervous, and that made me start telling my story really badly. "I think—no,

43

I believe—that my great-great-grandfather killed a jeweller named Goldstein."

'"Your great-great grandfather, you say. How old is he?" he said, already showing sarcasm in his voice.

'"Well actually, he is dead," I replied.

'"When did he die?" he returned.

'"1913," I said. *If only he would listen to what I have to say instead of continually asking me questions,* I thought, *we might start to get somewhere.* "I believe he robbed Goldstein's shop and hid the loot in the coffin of Annie Philpot, who is buried in a grave in Hamwell."

'"Where did you acquire all this information?"

'"I dreamt it, but what I would like you to do is dig up the grave, retrieve the gold, and return it to the Goldstein family."

'"Of course you would, sir," the baboon said then put his giant hands on my shoulders and steered me to the front door, saying, "Run along home now before I nick you for wasting police time."

'I stood shell-shocked outside the police station thinking, *What on earth happened there, and why did I bother?* I made my way home, plonked myself on my bed, and started to work on plan B. The treatment that I had received from the baboon hardened my resolve. No more asking for advice, no more police stations, just straightforward action. *What is the worst that could happen to me?* I thought, *What are the possible scenarios? Number 1, I dig up the grave and there isn't any loot in it, and so I then fill it in again and nobody will ever know. Number 2, I dig up the grave and there is some loot in it, in which I would take it out, fill in the grave, take it to Jeff and Mary Goldstein, tell them the whole story, and beg their forgiveness for Arthur's crime and also ask their forgiveness for my deceit in wheedling my way into their confidence, even though my motives were honourable.* The one scenario that I hadn't bargained for was getting myself arrested. I bought myself a spade and a torch and a tyre lever to open the coffin with and went into our garden to practice on digging holes. Working at a steady pace, I found I could dig a hole 6' × 3' × 2' deep in about an hour. Assuming that I could work at that speed throughout the exercise, it would take me three hours to dig the hole, fifteen minutes to open the coffin, and a little less than two hours to render it back to as near as possible to its original state.'

Martin interrupted the story. 'Holy Moses, Peters, you seem to have thought of everything. Let's take a short break. I want to ring Portsmouth Police to confirm your story with William Sykes.'

Len, always the joker, chipped in, 'Ask him if he has a dog named Bull's Eye.'

Both the men got the joke immediately; however, Pam was left puzzled to why they both laughed. Martin returned to his office to phone the Portsmouth police, which gave Graham a chance to explain the connection between William Sykes and Bull's Eye.

Sykes picked up his phone. 'Portsmouth Police Station, Detective Sykes speaking.'

'Good afternoon, Detective. My name is Detective Martin Penn. I am stationed at Hamwell police station.'

'Okay, so what can I do for you?' came the less-than-friendly response Martin would usually expect to receive from a fellow officer.

Suspecting that Sykes might be a little economical with the truth if he felt his judgement was being questioned, Martin put his question slightly different than he was originally going to. 'I have got a young bloke in custody who says he wants to report a murder. When I asked him how he got his information, he said he had dreamt it. I also asked him where he lived. He replied "Portsmouth." "So why didn't you go into Portsmouth Police Station and report it?" I asked. He said he did. He said he spoke to you. What I think is that he is going around different police stations making a nuisance of himself, giving him a feeling of importance.'

'I remember him,' said Sykes. 'He never got past the front door with me. The idiot wanted me go and dig up a grave. I told him to stop wasting police time or I'd nick him. That soon got rid of him.'

'That is exactly what I am going to do, and thanks for your help.' Martin returned to the interview room and, for the first time, addressed his suspect by his first name. 'Well, Graham, it appears you have been telling the truth all along, and yes, Sykes is a baboon.'

'Do you want me to finish my story, or shall we leave it at that?'

'I for one would love to hear it,' said Pam, who seemed so relieved Graham was now being believed.

'You have come this far. It would be a shame not to hear the conclusion' said Len. Martin agreed.

'I was already to go on a minute's notice. I had decided to wait for the weather report to show a cloudy night for obvious reasons. Isn't it always the way, when you're waiting for something to happen quickly, it never does? We seemed to be in a prolonged period of clear skies for weeks. Eventually, there was a change in the weather. I told my mother that I was going to a party and would probably be late home, "so don't bother waiting up for me", I set off down the A3 at approximately 7 p.m. and arrived at Hamwell at 9 p.m. I hadn't expected to start digging until 11.30 p.m., so I found a fast food restaurant to while away the time. As the time ticked by, I began to get a little nervous, and by 11 p.m., I was in such a state I was all but ready to call the whole thing off. *Pull yourself together,* I told myself. *Remember what you told yourself earlier. What is the worst that could happen?* I drove to Spring Close and parked my car, took out my tools, and made my way to Annie Philpot's grave. My pre-planning in the art of grave digging showed me that I was going exactly according to plan. It was around 3 a.m. before I started to prise the coffin lid open. "I am so sorry to wake you up, Annie," I said, 'but I need to look under your skeleton." Can you imagine my delight and amazement on finding the loot? However, my euphoria was very short-lived. I think you can continue the story from there, Detective. Just one thing has puzzled me, Detective—how the devil did you know what I was doing?'

'Well, Graham, you were extremely unlucky, if somebody hadn't been walking through the cemetery at that unearthly hour of night and spotted what you were doing then phoned the station, you would have been home and dry.'

'That,' said Len, 'without exception, is the strangest defence of one's actions that I have ever had the pleasure of witnessing, and the strange thing is I believe every word you have said, Graham. Please don't spoil it now by saying you made the whole thing up.'

Pam agreed, saying she was fascinated.

Martin, however, kept his feet firmly on the ground, saying, 'Your account, Graham, has certainly got merit, but I will have to do a lot of cross-checking of your statement with various parties that you have mentioned that might or might not confirm your story. Can I ask you to stay local for a few days until I complete my enquiries?'

'Of course, I will book myself into the Ferryman Hotel.'

'That is excellent,' said Martin. 'Of course we still have the matter of disturbing a grave to think about, but if your story is the truth, and I suspect it is, I will probably let you off with a caution.'

'Officer, may I ask you a question?'

'Yes, Graham?'

'Could you advise me on what will happen to the loot? The reason I ask is that if you hadn't caught me, I was going to present it to Jeff and Mary Goldstein. I have this thought that my recurring dreams won't subside until Arthur Tidwell's DNA that I have inherited can rest in peace.'

'First, Graham, we must try and determine that it is the Goldstein's property. Who knows—it might belong to the Philpot family, but I promise you this: I will do everything possible to uncover the truth, but in the meantime, you are free to go. If you go to the front desk, the desk sergeant will phone your mother to come and pick you up. She is staying locally in the George Hotel. It's no more than ten minutes away.'

Len said he will also check out the legal position of the ownership of the loot and keep in touch with Graham on events as they unfolded. Martin and Len left together, heading to the canteen, leaving Pam and Graham in the interview room. Pam clasped Graham's hand. 'I am so pleased you are being released without charge, Graham, and I think your account of what you have been through is intriguing.' She leaned across and gave him a tender kiss on the cheek, saying, 'In a way, I am sorry it is over.'

'That is a strange thing to say, Pam,' he replied. 'Why do you say that?'

'It means that I will probably never see you again.'

'Please don't say that, Pam. I would love to see you again but in more congenial surroundings, not with you sitting opposite me trying to lock me up.'

Pam laughed out loud, then her face went all serious. 'Do you really mean it, Graham?'

'I am staying in Hamwell for a few days, and I can't think of a nicer person to spend my evenings with, but you won't get yourself into trouble with your boss, will you?'

'I will take a phrase from what you said earlier—what is the worst than can happen to me?'

This time, Graham laughed. 'That's my girl,' he said.

Pam's heart skipped a beat. Even at this early stage in their relationship, for Graham to call her 'my girl' seemed to give her a good feeling. What was it about this young man that turned her legs to jelly? What was it that excited her every time he spoke? She couldn't understand it at all, but nobody had ever had this effect on her before. *You have only known him a matter of a few hours, and already he is making you act like a silly girl. Pull yourself together*, she lectured herself, but she was being engulfed by something much stronger than reason, and the more she tried to apply common sense, the stronger the feelings became.

Pam escorted Graham to the reception desk. She proudly stated that Mr Peters was free to go.

The policeman manning the desk just tut-tutted in a way that said quite clearly that he, for one, didn't consider him innocent.

Pam immediately picked up on his snide tone. 'Mr Peters is innocent, so I would be obliged if you would keep your thoughts to yourself and sound a little less vindictive. You know nothing about him, and your opinions are not welcome, so if you would be kind enough to return Mr Peters's belongings to him, we would be most grateful. And I believe Mr Peters's mother has left her mobile number with you, so if you would kindly ring her and ask her to pick up her son, we would be very much obliged.'

'Right away, Constable.' The sergeant might have outranked her, but there was no way he was getting into a confrontation with this little vixen.

Graham couldn't believe what he had just witnessed.

Pam sat with Graham on the reception chairs to await his mother's arrival, 'Christ, Pam,' he whispered, 'What was that all about?'

'He knows nothing about you whatsoever, Graham, and I resented the implication in his tone. You are a good man who deserves a little more respect.'

'Wow! I am sure glad you are on my side.'

It seemed just a few minutes had transpired before his mother stepped through the door. She immediately spotted her son sitting, waiting for her. 'Come on,' she said in a very forthright way. 'Let us get as far away from here as possible.'

'Okay! Mother, calm down, let me just thank Constable Turner for her treatment of me.' He turned around and looked at Pam. 'Thank you, Constable,' he said. 'I will not forget the support you have given me, and who knows? We might meet again.' He gave her an encouraging wink then turned around and left with his mother. They made their way straight back to her room at the George Hotel. She made them both coffee then sat down beside him.

'Right, let's hear it then.' The tone of her voice spoke volumes about her mood. 'What on earth have you been up to? Have you gone out of your mind?'

'Calm down, Mother, I guess I have quite a lot of explaining to do, but first, may I say I am sorry for all the trouble I have caused you?'

'So you should be, son. You have had me worried out of my mind.'

'Where shall I start? Do you remember me saying to you that I had a strange dream earlier this year?'

'Vaguely.'

'Well the dream kept returning night after night. Three names appeared in my dreams: Arthur Tidwell, Annie Philpot—she always appeared in a coffin—and the name Goldstein. It got so bad that at one stage I seriously thought of seeking professional help.'

'Why didn't you tell me, son?'

'I did. You told me not to eat cheese before bedtime. Actually, Mother, it was you who set me off on this crazy quest.'

'Me? Oh, I thought it would be my fault.'

'No, Mother, it's not your fault. What I mean is this. Do you remember asking me to accompany you to visit Gran and I said "no thanks", but you finally persuaded me to go with you? Well, it was at Gran's that I found out that Arthur Tidwell was actually my great-great-grandfather? I also discovered that he committed suicide and died bearing a terrible secret, and that is what got me started.'

'But how did you end up digging up a grave up in Hamwell?'

'Now that is a long story. Are you sure you want to hear it?'

'Yes, but not now. It's time we headed back to Portsmouth.'

'Sorry, Mother, you go, but I have to stay here for a few days until they check my story out.'

'Just you keep me informed of your situation?' That little telltale tear appeared in her eye again as she put her arms around him.

'You can do one thing for me, Mother.'

'What is that, son?'

'Can you give me a lift to where I left my car? I hope it is still there.'

He helped his mother to gather up the few things that she came with. They walked down to reception together, where she checked out. She then drove him to Spring Close where his car was still parked, much to his relief. Another hug from his mother, then they parted company.

'You will keep me informed of what is happening, Graham, won't you?' she said, popping her head out of the car window.

'Of course, Mother, don't worry, and please drive safely.'

She drove away, putting her arm out of the window and waving as she disappeared around the corner.

He turned around, fumbled for his keys, and pointed them at his car. The lights flashed, indicating that the doors had unlocked. He sat himself down in the driver's seat and, before starting the engine, paused for a moment, recalling all that had happened to him. Looking back, it all seemed unreal, bizarre even. He wondered how it was all going to end. He thought about the person that had caused all this trouble, then he spoke his name out loud to himself. 'Arthur Tidwell, why did you have to be my great-great-granddad?' Then with one turn of the key, he was heading back to his hotel.

CHAPTER SEVEN

Friday night and Martin was relieved that it was his last night shift for a whole month. He was sitting at his desk, jotting down the people he needed to visit to confirm Graham's story. *I will do the local ones first thing tomorrow morning*, he thought. *First Jeff and Mary Goldstein, then the solicitors Smithers and Son, and finally, the Long Boat. If his alibi holds up, then next week, my first visit will be to Graham's gran. I don't think I have her address. I will have to ask Graham for that*, he thought, *and while I'm at it, where I can get hold of Professor Irvin?* He had just finished his rota for next week when the door opened, and Dave Harris walked in. Martin looked up. 'Hello, Dave, are you feeling better?'

'Not too bad, Martin. I think I had a dodgy curry. Has anything exciting happening?'

Martin, not wanting to let Dave anywhere near Graham's case, played it down casually saying, 'Not a lot Dave.'

'How did you get on with Peter's?'

Martin was sensing that Dave was pumping him for information, 'I've just got a few loose ends to tie up before I make a decision to charge him or not.'

Dave could sense Martin was not going to give him the whole story so decided to let the subject drop. 'Right, I will see you later.'

'Sure thing, Dave, and it's good to see you back.' The door closed behind Dave. Martin mumbled to himself, 'You are not getting your hands on this one, mate.' Although he was itching to get started, Martin decided not to start his enquiries the following morning but to resume on Monday morning. It was still only half an hour into his Friday night shift. He picked up the phone and rang Pam.

She was lying on her bed when it rang, and her heart skipped a beat. 'Hello. Pam speaking.'

'Pam, I know it's late, and I do apologise. I don't suppose you have got Graham Peters's phone number?'

'Yes, I have, sir'

'I thought you might have.'

'What do you mean, sir?'

'Come on, Pam, I'm a detective. I've seen the way you look at each other, but don't worry, your secret is safe with me.'

'Thank you, sir, that's very kind of you, but I'm not sure my feelings are being reciprocated.'

'Never mind, Pam. Anyway, thanks for the phone number, and keep your pecker up, oh ye of little faith.'

'You're right as usual, sir, good night.'

Martin felt sad for this young lovebird, so he changed his mind and immediately phoned Graham. He was in luck Graham hadn't retired to bed yet. 'Graham, this is Detective Martin Penn speaking. Could you supply me with your grandmother's address please? Also, where I can get hold of Professor Irvin?' After Graham had given Martin the information he required, he said, 'Oh, just one other thing—there is a little lady we both know who is waiting anxiously by her phone for someone to ring her, and it's not me.'

Graham laughed. 'Message received and understood. I will call her tomorrow morning.'

Martin's night shift had come to an end. 'Two glorious days off,' he said to himself. He had asked his wife, Gloria, to stock up the camper van because he wanted to get as far away from Hamwell police station as possible. There was a little camp site about seventy miles outside of London heading north up the AIM that they liked, a massive reservoir that stored Anglia Waters's water supply. They were both keen cyclists, and Grafham Waters had a cycle path circling its entire perimeter. He was a keen fisherman, and the waters were regularly stocked with trout, and Gloria loved to cook a trout on the barbecue. They arrived at Grafham at 9.30 p.m. Gloria poured them both a beer, and by 11 p.m., Martin was dead to the world. The weather was favourable; he could recharge his batteries and be all refreshed for Monday morning. Sunday morning, he hired a day boat to fish the waters. Fishing was a wonderful way to relax and ponder the world and all its problems, as he was sitting in the middle of the lake, his mind started to think about Graham. 'Why do I not want to charge him? Why do I want to believe that everything he has told me is the truth, and if it is the truth, it could have far-reaching consequences for the legal profession, could the inherited thoughts of a dead person be submitted as evidence?' He thought that the way Graham had explained, it made complete sense to him. His line went taut, and it wasn't long before dinner, a very nice rainbow trout. He continued to fish for another hour without success, so he started up the outboard motor and proudly headed back to the fishing lodge, eager for the hunter to present his catch to his mate.

Saturday night back in Hamwell, another young buck was trying to impress a potential mate. Graham had taken the hint and phoned Pam that morning and invited her to dine with him at the Ferryman; she had been on cloud nine all day and made a particular effort with her make-up. When she walked into the Ferryman, Graham looked stunned at her beauty. He had only ever seen her in her uniform; this was a different Pam altogether. He led her to the table and took her coat, then pulled the chair out for her. He then sat down opposite and handed her the menu. She was impressed; the young men she normally dated were a pint of lager and a packet of crisps.

They talked all evening. she thought he would invite her up to his room afterwards and she would have gone willingly, but he never did. He did walk her back to her car. He told her he was so glad that they had met and would phone her in the morning; he then kissed her and said goodbye. She asked if they could meet up tomorrow night; he said yes. They were both unaware of it, but the seeds of love had been planted.

Monday morning arrived, and Martin was itching to get started. He realised he didn't have the Goldsteins' address, so another quick phone call to Graham was required. 'Graham, it's Detective Penn again. I hope I haven't woken you up, but I need the Goldsteins' address. After Graham had furnished him with the information, his curiosity got the better of him. 'Did you have a good weekend?'

'Excellent, thank you officer,'

'Message received and understood.' Martin said.

They both laughed then ended the call. He phoned into the station to update them of his whereabouts and headed straight for the Goldsteins' house. Jeff opened the door, still in his pyjamas. 'Whatever you're selling, we don't want it,' he grunted.

'That's good, because I am not selling. I am a police officer, Mr Goldstein, and I need to ask you a few questions.'

'What about?' Jeff inquired suspiciously.

'Don't panic. I am not here to arrest you. I don't like talking on the doorstep. Do you think we might go inside?'

'Yeah, but just hold on a sec. Mary, are you decent?' he shouted down the hallway.

'Yes, why?' came the reply.

'There is a policeman here, and he wants to ask us some questions.'

55

'What about?'

'I don't know.'

'Well, bring him in. We have nothing to hide.'

Jeff led Martin into the lounge. They both sat on the settee, and Martin gave the room a quick scan, and his first impression was that this young couple were finding life pretty tough.

'Mr Goldstein, I am making enquiries about a man with the same surname as you who owned a jeweller's in Broad Street, and I wondered if he might have been related to you, and if so, do you have any information that might help me in my enquiries? He was murdered in 1911.'

Jeff looked at Martin suspiciously then rested his arms on his hip and spoke.

'Okay, what's going on? You are the second person to be interested in my great-great-granddad. Did you hear that, Mary? He is asking questions about my great-great-granddad?'

Mary came to the door. 'Is this anything to do with Graham Peters?' she said.

'I don't know a Graham Peters. What did he want?' She had answered one of his questions that he felt unable to ask without implicating Graham in his enquiries.

'He was researching the history of Broad Street,' Mary boasted. 'He bought the twins both a teddy bear and a box of chocolates for me.'

'Sorry, I haven't got any gifts. What we are doing is going over cold cases—that is to say, cases we have not had a satisfactory conclusion to. Has anything been handed down from generations that you feel might be of any use to us?'

'The only thing that the robbing B_____ has handed down to my family was hardship and poverty. Your guys nearly caught him, you know, but he gave you the slip.'

'What about the stolen goods? Did you ever find out what happened to them?'

'No, they were never seen again,' said Jeff.

'I know this might seem like we are wasting our time, Mr and Mrs Goldstein, but you would be surprised how often a little snippet of information can start the ball rolling again. Anyway, thank you for your time. I will see myself out.' He left the Goldsteins with the same mixed feelings as Graham had—anger at how one act of greed can leave a lasting impression a hundred years later, and a feeling that he also would like to change this family's fortunes.

He made his way to the town centre, taking the same route that Graham had said that he had taken, through the High Street, turning left into Broad Street. He hesitated and looked both up and down the road, observing the mixture of the old and the new buildings. He so much wanted to feel the feeling of déjà vu that Graham had experienced, but alas—nothing. Starting at the Mews, he walked to the wall that ran along one side. He jumped up and leaned over. He saw the three outhouses circling the old courtyard. He jumped down and made his way to the front of the property. Looking up at the sign above, it read 'Smithers and Son'. Without hesitation, he walked through the door.

'Good morning, sir, how may I help you?' came the well-rehearsed introduction.

One thing I can say about Graham Peters, he thought, *is he sure shows attention to detail when he recites his events.* 'My name is DI Martin Penn from Hamwell police station. I wish to speak to a Mr Smithers, please?'

'I will phone through to see if he is available,' she said, sounding quite worried. 'He will see you now, sir, the first floor then the second door on the right.'

He walked up the narrow staircase catching the ingrained smell of age that Graham had also noticed. He knocked on Smithers's door.

'Enter?' came the official-sounding reply.

Martin entered his office. It was like walking into another world. *This guy is a real gadget man*, he thought, *and he must be PC World's best customer.*

'Good morning, sir. My name is DI Penn. I won't take up too much of your time, so I will come straight to the point. I believe a young man visited you a while ago, claiming to be from the local gazette?'

'Yes, that is correct.'

'Can you tell me what he wanted?'

'He said he was researching the history of Broad Street and asked if I could tell him if Smithers had been the first business to occupy the property. He was particularly interested in the turn of the last century. I told him no, we were not'

'And who did own the shop then?' Martin probed.

'I couldn't remember at first. It was only when he was halfway out of the door that I remembered it was an undertaker's. I don't know why, but he seemed delighted with the news.'

'Thank you for your time, Mr Smithers. That is all I wish to know.'

'Can you tell me what this is all about, Officer?'

'I can't, sir. I'm sorry, but it is part of an ongoing investigation, but thank you again.' Martin left the building and headed towards the Long Boat Inn. He ordered a coffee and drank it, viewing the pictures on the wall. A really old brown photograph hung there, showing a parade of shops including Goldstein's, the jewellers and goldsmith. That completed the morning's checking. Deciding to leave the visit to Graham's gran and Professor Irvin until the morning. He made his way back to the police station. He walked into his office, plonked himself behind his desk, and picked up his mail: an invitation to attend a senior detectives' training seminar, a letter from the local council enquiring into to whom they should send the bill for filling in Annie Philpot's grave (£180 plus VAT)—*Cripes, I'm in the wrong business*, he thought—and a memo from the chief superintendent reminding him he was late with his reports. He rang the council and forwarded Graham's particulars then phoned Graham to give him a warning that a nasty little surprise was heading his way in the post. Then he half-heartedly filled in a couple of reports on trivial crimes that he had solved—a stolen car (it turned out the owner had left it down the pub but was too drunk to remember he had driven there, so he had walked the five miles home) and the break in at the local bookie's (it turned out to be an ex-employee who had been sacked, not so much a break in because he had had a duplicate key made). He strolled down to the chief's office; his door was open.

'Come in, Martin. I can see you have read my memo.' He looked at the reports in Martin's hand. 'Sit down a moment and tell me about the dreamer that everyone is talking about.'

'Let me surprise you, Chief. I believe every word he has told me.'

'Really?'

'Really, sir, I have checked every bit of information he has given me, and I can't find a single discrepancy. I've got two more visits to make tomorrow, and that should finish my investigations. This case that started out so easy to solve, just maybe the biggest case this station has ever handled.'

'How do you arrive at that conclusion, Martin?'

'Well, Chief, if Peters's great-great-grandfather did pass on his memories through his DNA, that could have far-reaching implications for the legal profession.'

'Yes, I can see that, Martin,' said the chief, scratching his chin.

'He is no fool, sir. He is a biological scientist who works with a team of scientists searching for cures for cancers. If—as I suspect they will—my investigations tomorrow will back up his story, then I will let him off with a caution for disturbing the grave.'

'I look forward to reading your report, Martin, and I am sure you will do the right thing.'

'Thank you, sir, I will.'

'Don't bother closing the door on your way out. I like to hear what's going on out there.'

He left the chief's office feeling whatever he put in his report on Graham Peters, it would get an honest appraisal.

Returning to his office to plan Tuesday's investigations, he found himself once again lacking the information he needed to complete his enquiries, and once again he found himself ringing Graham, 'Hello, Graham, I am going to visit your gran tomorrow and also Professor Irvin. I need the addresses and phone numbers, please, if you have them. I don't want to drive all that way and find that she has gone shopping for the day.'

Graham supplied Martin with his granny's phone number and address, but the professor's home address he didn't have.

'Sorry, Officer, I only have his office phone number. You can find him at Hermes Research Centre, Flitch Street, Portsmouth.'

'I hope to conclude my investigations by tomorrow evening, so if you could come into the station Wednesday morning, we can discuss what action I am going to take.'

'Thank you, Officer.'

'Are you still having the dreams, Graham?' Martin enquired.

'Every night,' Graham replied, 'but at least I have somebody else to dream about now.'

'That's great, Graham. I will see you Wednesday morning.' He phoned Graham's gran and the professor and made an appointment to see both of them then called it a day.

Grandma had got up early Wednesday morning. She had tidied up then popped down to her local shop. She purchased a packet of biscuits and a small box of fondant fancies to offer Martin when he arrived. Every five minutes, she glanced out of the window. It was 10.30 a.m. before a car she never recognised pulled into the close. She quickly jumped into action, kettle on,

Do You Believe in Life After Death?

biscuits on a plate, cling film off the fondant fancies, all before Martin pulled into the driveway.

He introduced himself, saying, 'You must be Graham's gran?' He gave his usual bit of flattery, commenting on the beautiful area where she lived and that she looked a lot younger than he imagined. That seemed to do the trick.

'Come in, young man, I have just put the kettle on.' She led him into the lounge. 'Tea or coffee?'

'Coffee, please.'

'Help yourself to a biscuit, there on the table,' she said, then brought in the coffee and fondant fancies on a tray. 'Now what has my grandson been up to?'

'Some time ago, he visited you with his mother and he told you he was having disturbing dreams. Can you confirm that?'

'Yes, I can,' she said. 'One of the people in his dreams had the same name as my granddad, Arthur Tidwell.'

'That was my next question. What can you tell me about Arthur Tidwell?'

'I never knew him, but according to my gran, he was a nasty piece of work. I think she was glad to see the back of him.'

'Why was that?'

'He was a big man with a violent temper, not a lot upstairs, if you know what I mean, so he liked to do his talking with his fists. He committed suicide, you know. He died a troubled soul.'

'So Graham has told me. He also told me that he had left a suicide note.'

'Yes, that is true. I have it in a box in the cupboard under the stairs.'

'If it isn't too much trouble, would you mind if I saw it? It is just to verify Graham's story. You do understand, don't you?'

'Of course I do, young man. I will get it for you right now. Do help yourself to a fondant fancy.' She returned with the Sunlight soap box and rummaged around in it until she pulled out the note.

61

'This is the note, Officer.' She handed it to Martin, who read it, confirming once again Graham's account of the note.

'Would you have any objections if I kept the note as evidence?'

'Not at all, young man, but I can't see for the life of me what good it is to you.'

'Well, obviously you won't now, but next time you see your grandson, ask him about it. I think you will find his story fascinating.'

'I will,' she said. 'It sounds fascinating.'

'Thank you for your time, ma'am. I think I have covered everything.'

'Please have another cup of coffee before you go,' she begged.

'Very well, ma'am, you really are most kind.' A cup of coffee and two fondant fancies later and he finally managed to escape. He arrived in Portsmouth at 2.15 p.m. Thanks to his satnav, he never wasted any time finding Flitch Street, and the Hermes Research Centre sign was so large it was unmissable to anybody driving down the road looking for it. The front gate was manned by a guard who checked visitors in and operated a barrier. Martin introduced himself and gave him the name of the person he was visiting. The guard directed him to the car park and pointed to the reception door he required.

'You will need a visitor's badge to get into the building proper. They will give you one at reception,' he explained. 'I will phone through to let them know you are on your way.'

He parked up and made his way to reception. He rang the bell, and almost immediately, another guard opened it.

'Are you Detective Penn?' he asked.

Martin showed him his warrant card. The guard gave it a longer-than-necessary scan and then allowed him into the building, and he then gave Martin a visitor's badge and told him to take a seat while he contacted Professor Irvin.

Do You Believe in Life After Death?

The intercom blasted out, 'Could Professor Irvin contact reception please?'

Martin commented to the guard, 'Your security is very tight in here, isn't it?'

'Yes it is,' said the guard. 'We can't have any old Tom, Dick, or Harry strolling around willy-nilly.' The phone rang; the guard picked up the receiver, 'Professor, I have a police officer here. He says he has an appointment to see you. Very good, sir.'

He stepped out from behind the reception desk and instructed Martin to follow him; he followed him, feeling like a school boy being led to the headmaster for the cane. The guard knocked on the Professor's office door, the professor opened the door and thanked the guard, then beckoned Martin in. He was a big man, a man who enjoyed his food judging by his rather expanded waist, he sported union jack braces a white shirt and a polka dot bow tie that made him the perfect candidate for the nutty professor award.

'What can I do for you detective?'

'Graham Peter's sir, I believe he works for you?'

'That is correct, although I've had to stand him down temporarily while he sorts himself out.'

'Why is that sir?'

'We are a team here, and he was letting his problems affect the team's performance.'

'Do you know what his problems were?' Martin probed.

'He said he was experiencing some vivid dreams and had a theory that a distant relative had committed a crime and was contacting him through his inherited DNA. He said he thought his great- great-grandfather might have robbed somebody and was asking Graham to return the stolen loot to its rightful owner. I was very reluctant to step him down from the team. He has a brilliant mind, and I see no reason whatsoever why he can't reach the top of the tree in his chosen field of research. I asked him if he knew where the loot was hidden. He said he didn't.'

'He does now,' said Martin.

'What do you mean?' asked the professor.

'We arrested him in a grave that he had dug up. He was holding a bag of gold and silver.' All of a sudden, the professor's whole demeanour changed. He lit up, putting his thumbs inside his braces and giving them a twang. 'Let me guess,' he said excitedly, as though it was a game, 'the person whose grave it was in, was it Annie Philpot?'

'Yes it was,' said Martin, 'but how did you know?'

'The very last words I spoke to him were that Annie Philpot sounds like she has more secrets to give up.'

'He did tell us everything you just told me, Professor, I hope you can appreciate that I needed to hear it from you to confirm his story.'

'Of course. It is how we work here—we question everything.'

'Thank you for your time, Professor.'

'Give Graham my regards when you see him, and tell him I am looking forward to him returning to work.'

'I will, sir. Thank you again. I will see myself out.'

'Oh no you won't, Detective, I will call for an escort,' he said in a firm but light-hearted way.

The escort knocked on the door. Martin shook the professor's hand and said 'Goodbye.'

The professor, however, never said goodbye but just shook his head, saying, 'What a clever little so-and-so. He has figured it out. I am delighted for him. Maybe he can finally get his life back together.'

Martin drove back to London. He had no doubt in his mind now that Graham's account of his story was the truth and that there was no way he would charge him for his little misdemeanour of digging up Annie's grave. He arrived back in his office at 4.15 p.m. He called Len to arrange an appointment for the following morning with his client. Len agreed to come. 'Shall we say 10 a.m.?' They agreed on the time, and Len immediately phoned Graham.

Martin sat back in his chair. He felt a strong feeling of contentment. He was beginning to feel a respect for Graham, not just because everything that he had told him appeared to be the truth, but he had also furnished him with the most interesting case of his career.

CHAPTER EIGHT

The following morning, Martin sat in his office, awaiting the arrival of Graham and Len. He was feeling quite proud of himself. Even though he hadn't charged Graham, he felt he had achieved the correct outcome to the strangest case he ever had the pleasure to investigate. He was certainly going to claim the credit for solving the murder of Mr Goldstein and the retrieving of the stolen loot. Len and Graham turned up bang on time. They said their good mornings and sat down on the two chairs that Martin had borrowed from the canteen.

'I won't beat about the bush, Graham. I have concluded my investigation and have spoken to everyone you mentioned in your statement, and I am pleased to inform you that unless there is a great conspiracy to which I am the only person not privy, they all confirm everything you told me. The Goldsteins, Smithers, the photograph on the wall of the Long Boat, your gran—a lovely woman, she must have thought I looked undernourished because she couldn't stop feeding me cake.'

Len and Graham both laughed.

'Then there was the nutty professor. He seemed positively overjoyed when I told him that I arrested you down a grave with a bag of gold in your hand. By the way, he sends his regards and is looking forward to seeing you back at work.'

'That is great news,' said Len.

'So I am pleased to inform you that I won't be charging you with anything today, but I will be cautioning you for digging up a grave without permission. Even if the baboon had done his job properly, I wouldn't even be doing that.'

Len patted Graham on the back and said, 'You can get back to a normal life now, Graham. You must be quite relieved with the outcome.'

'Relieved, yes. Happy, no. You seem to be forgetting how I arrived in this situation in the first place. I was—and still am—having haunting dreams that are affecting my life, and I don't think they are going to go away until Arthur Tidwell has righted the wrong that he has done to the Goldsteins all those years ago.'

'You honestly think that that will cure your torment?' said Martin.

'I am convinced that is the only way that I will get peace of mind.'

'It will take time, Graham, but if Len and myself can make a case for handing the loot over to the rightful owner, then we might stand a reasonable chance of succeeding. I think we can show beyond doubt that it is indeed the property of the Goldsteins, but in the meantime, try and put it out of your mind and enjoy life.'

'I suppose you will be heading home to Portsmouth now?' said Len.

'No, I will return back home this weekend. I have somebody I want to say goodbye to first.'

Martin knew exactly who Graham was referring to but said nothing.

He said his goodbyes and left the station. He had intended to go to the Goldsteins' but had second thoughts; he phoned Pam to tell her the news.

'Please don't go home before I see you?' she pleaded.

'Of course I won't. I have decided to stay until the weekend because I want to see as much of you as possible.'

'Me too,' she replied.

'I don't know what I will do, not being able to see you every night, darling,' he said.

'That is the first time you have called me that, Graham.'

'Called you what, Pam?'

'Darling.'

'Is it? It just rolled off my tongue, it seemed so natural.'

'I like it when you call me that, Graham. So where shall we meet tonight?'

'I feel like celebrating with a meal at the Ferryman—unless there is anything else you fancy doing?'

'That sounds perfect, dear. I will meet you at 8 p.m. I love you,' she whispered.

'I love you too. I'll see you at eight, bye.'

Martin finished his report on Graham's case then took it down the corridor to the chief superintendent's office. The door was wide open as usual, but the chief super wasn't in. Martin went in and placed the report on the desk. He scribbled a note, asking the chief to contact him after reading it, saying he would welcome his advice on how to proceed regarding the stolen goods. Returning to his office, he then phoned Len.

'Len, this is Martin Penn, regarding Graham Peters. I really want to see his theory through to its final conclusion, i.e. the contents of the robbery being returned to the Goldstein family.'

'I am sure between us we can make a good case based on what I would say is indisputable evidence, Martin. I have already spoken to a friend of mine, she is a judge. I explained the circumstances of the case to her and the importance of releasing the loot ASAP. Her first reaction was that I was joking, but when I finally convinced her that I was deadly serious, she said that I would have an impossible task trying to convince a court of the validity of the story because if the court agrees with your conclusions, then they must conclude that it is indeed possible for the thought DNA of a dead person to be passed on to future generations, and if they concede that, then that would make that kind of evidence admissible in court, and that takes it to a whole new level. Her advice was don't even go there—it could drag on for years.

'Yes, Len, I can see that. I feel I owe it to Peters to try and give him peace of mind. I must admit he is a likeable lad.'

'Martin, you are getting soft in your old age,' Len joked. 'By the way, I have been making inquiries into the Philpot family. Annie and Joe Philpot were married in 1893. Joe listed his occupation as a chimney sweep, and Annie, a scullery maid. They had one child, a girl. She died at nineteen years old, one year after her mother,'

'What did she die of?' asked Martin.

'She drowned in a boating accident. Joe signed up to fight in the First World War and was killed in action in 1916, and that is all I could find out about the Philpotses.'

'I think, based on what you have just told me, we can safely assume the loot didn't belong to them. Thanks for that information, Len, and if you uncover anything else, please let me know.'

It was two days later before the chief superintendent contacted Martin. He had left a message on his desk, asking to see him in his office as soon as he came in. Martin had been called out to a house burglary. An old couple had returned home to be greeted by a broken window in the side door, and their house had been turned upside down. They didn't have a lot, so the arsehole who had robbed them had probably only got away with enough to buy the next fix. It was the distress he inflicted on the old couple that Infuriated Martin. There were three or four suspects he knew of who were low enough to commit this crime, and he was confident he would arrest the culprit by the weekend. Arriving back in his office, he sat down and picked up the note from his in tray, he picked up the phone and rang the super, 'I've just returned, Chief. Are you free to see me now?'

'Yes, I am, Martin. I want to discuss the Peters report with you,'

'Give me five minutes, sir, I will just have a quick cup of coffee, then I will be in to see you.'

'Get two cups and bring them to my office. Mine is two sugars.'

Martin laughed, saying, 'You don't miss a trick, do you?'

'That is why I am where I am and you are where you are. Now go and get the coffees.'

Martin had a good rapport with the chief super and was confident he could get a fair hearing, no matter what crazy conclusions he might arrive at, and the Peters case didn't come any crazier from a detective's point of view.

'Close the door after you, Martin, and take a chair, and let us run through this report together. I don't mind telling you it takes a bit of believing.'

'I totally agree, Chief, and I don't mind telling you that I had quite a struggle writing it, but I am convinced that it is the truth. I have checked every single aspect of Peter's account of events, and every word was confirmed by the people I interviewed, even the detective in Portsmouth Station, the one Peters calls the baboon, confirmed his story, and quite honestly I think Peters description of Detective Sykes wasn't far short of the truth.'

'What is he like, this Peters?'

'Well, Chief, he is twenty-seven years old, well educated, he comes from a stable background. His boss, Professor Irvin, talks very highly of him, saying he shows great potential. Very polite, and the examples he gave of the theory of what is happening to him made complete sense.'

'Give me an example, Martin.'

'In an attempt to get the point across that he had inherited his great-great-grandfather's DNA, he gave an example of a cuckoo and how it instinctively knows that immediately after it has hatched, it has to throw all remaining eggs out of the nest, claiming the only way that the cuckoo chick could know this would be if it had inherited thought DNA from its parents. He gave three examples and then went on to talk about the feeling of déjà vu that he experienced when he walked into Broad Street. He asked if any of us had experienced the feeling, and I had to admit that I had. Whatever Graham Peters is, he is no fake or criminal.'

'My word, Martin. He has made an impression on you,' said the chief.

'Yes, he has, and another thing, he intended returning the stolen goods to its rightful owners, the Goldstein family, and I now intend to help him in any way I can to achieve his objective. I spoke to Len Brown today. He is Peters's solicitor. He has been making enquiries into Annie Philpot and her family, and there are no surviving relatives. When they were alive, they were of a lowly station, so the chances of the gold being theirs is pretty remote. Peters is still experiencing these haunting dreams, he is convinced the only way he can rid himself of his terrible dreams is to put right the wrong that he feels the DNA of his ancestor is begging him to do.'

'Cripes, Martin, spooky. I would like to meet this extraordinary young man.'

'I believe he is still in town until the end of the week, sir. I will see if I can arrange it. One other thing, sir—if you accept that he is telling the truth, we can claim a result for the solving of a cold case robbery and murder in 1911.'

'Ask him to pop into the police station before he heads back home, because if you want me to sign up for the crusade, I need to be confident in my own mind that he is genuine.'

'Thanks, Chief, I will contact him right away.' He left the chief's office with his spirits raised. Heading for his office, he bumped into Pam Turner.

'Good afternoon, sir,' she sang out.

'Hello, Pam, you sound happy. Are you still in contact with Graham?'

'Oh yes, sir.'

'Will you ask him to come in to see me tomorrow morning at 10 a.m.?'

'Can I ask why, sir?'

'The chief super has taken an interest in his case, and I have convinced him that Graham has told us the truth, and if Graham can convince him, then he will use his authority to get the gold released so Graham can complete his quest.'

'Thank you, sir, it sounds as if you have been converted.'

'Do you know, Pam, I believe I have.'

She gave Martin a hug then skipped up the corridor like a spring chicken. Unable to contain her excitement, she phoned Graham. 'Hello, sweetheart, I have some brilliant news for you. Martin wants to see you in his office at 10 a.m. tomorrow. The chief superintendent has taken an interest in your case, and if you can convince him that your story is the truth, he will do his uttermost to get the gold released for you to present to the Goldsteins.'

'Easier said than done, love. Do you remember the job I had convincing your boss the last time?'

'Come on, darling, this doesn't sound like you. I just know you can do it.'

'Sorry, but I had a particularly vivid dream last night. I think Arthur is getting restless.'

'We are all on your side, darling, so don't despair.'

'If only that person hadn't spotted me in the cemetery, I could have taken the loot, given it back to the Goldsteins, and nobody would have been any the wiser.'

'You are forgetting one thing, Graham.'

'What is that, Pam?'

'We would never have met.'

'Perhaps Arthur Tidwell was not such a bad man after all. Anyway, thanks for the information, and I will see you later.'

The following morning, Martin waited in his office for Graham to arrive. It was 9.55 a.m., just enough time for him to slip out for a cigarette. No sooner had he lit up when Graham's car pulled into the car park. He was halfway through his cigarette when Graham approached him. Graham spoke first. 'My work involves finding cures for cancers, and one of the main causes of cancer is smoking.'

'You're beginning to sound like my wife, young man.' He stubbed his cigarette in the tray provided and beckoned Graham into the police station. He opened his office door, letting Graham enter first, then he followed, closing the door behind him.

They both sat down, and Martin began to tell Graham what had transpired between himself and the chief superintendent.

'You know by now, Graham, that I, Pam, and Len are completely behind you, and we are doing everything we can to get the loot released early so that you can finish what you have started, but from our level we can only do so much. The chief super has taken a personal interest in your case, and he wishes to see you. In effect, he wants you to convince him that you are not some con artist. Do you think you can do that? If you can, it should speed up the releasing process considerably.'

'I will give it my best shot, Martin, but I can only tell him what I have told you already.'

'You have nothing to lose and a lot to gain, Graham. Just be yourself and confident and let the facts speak for themselves, okay?'

'All right, let's do it. It's a bit short notice, but hey, what the heck—in for a penny, in for a pound.'

'That's the spirit, my boy, onwards and upwards,' said Martin encouragingly. 'I will ring through now and see if he is available.'

The chief picked up the phone.

'Martin here, Chief. I have Graham Peters in my office. Are you free to see him?'

'I am a little tied up at the moment. I should be free in one hour. Take him to the canteen for a coffee, and I will see you and him at 11.30 a.m.' Martin obeyed his instruction and led Graham to the canteen. They sat chatting.

Martin seemed more nervous than Graham. 'Have you given any thought to how you will lay out your case?' he asked, knowing that if he couldn't convince the chief of his truthfulness, then the likelihood of the loot being released early was extremely slim.

Graham replied that he would just let the conversation take its own course, which didn't calm Martin's nerves one iota.

Martin then enquired about how he and Pam were progressing.

Graham said that he hoped their relationship was not going to fizzle out once he returned home, but he would have to get back to work soon—that is, if Professor Irvin would take him back.

At 11.25, they walked down to the chief super's office. Martin introduced them to each other.

'Sit down, Martin.' Turning his attention to Graham, he said, 'So you are the lad that is causing all the excitement in the station. Please take a seat and make yourself comfortable.' He had a folder in front of him. He opened it, then tapped his finger on to it, indicating that it was Martin's report.

'I have read the report that Martin has drafted, and its believability is challenging, to say the least, but Martin, whom I have a lot of respect for as a detective, seems utterly convinced that your account of how you ended up here is the truth. Now you tell me why I shouldn't treat you like some common thief or conman?'

'Well, sir, as you have just said, my story is—how did you put it—lacking in believability. I actually said that myself when I was interviewed. I even asked them not to allow me any visitors until after I gave my evidence, purely because I didn't want to be accused of leaking evidence out to a third party. I suppose I was so desperate to unload all that I had discovered that in a way it was a relief to get it off my chest. My first plan when I had formed a theory as to what was being transmitted to me through my great-great-grandfather's DNA was to go to the police in Portsmouth and ask if they would dig up the grave to confirm my theory, but I was treated as a joke.'

'Ah,' said the chief, 'that would be the baboon.'

'I have confirmed that Graham did indeed speak to Detective Sykes, the baboon,' said Martin.

'DNA, sir—that is what this is all about,' said Graham. 'I can see by that photograph on your desk that your DNA has been passed on to your next generation. Tell me, sir, are they your children?'

'Yes, they are.'

'Well, can you see where I am going with this? Taking it a step further, is it possible that your DNA that contains your thoughts could also be passed on? In my case—and bear in mind this is still just theory—I believe Arthur Tidwell, my great-great-grandfather, robbed and murdered a Mr Goldstein. He was caught in the act by the police, who gave chase but lost him. He hid in the undertaker's and hid the loot in Annie Philpot's open coffin then went home when the coast was clear, and the vivid, fearful memory of what he experienced on that fateful day lived in his mind until the day that he committed suicide. He fathered a child between committing the crime and his suicide, and that child was my great-grandmother, and she was the host for the DNA transfer.'

'We do have a record of the police report on the robbery and murder of Mr Goldstein, and it concurs with everything Graham has said,' said Martin.

'When all this is over, I intend to research thought transference in DNA and write a paper on the subject.'

After Graham had made his case, the chief picked up the photo of his children and studied it for a good thirty seconds then looked at Martin and, with a kind of shoulder shrug, conceded the argument. 'Graham,' he sighed, 'I have heard you out, and the opinion that I have formed of you is that you are no con man but a man who speaks his mind with conviction. However, you should not have disturbed that grave. We do all live in a law-abiding country, although in your case, after your encounter with our representative in Portsmouth, the baboon, I think the less said about that, the better, so you can consider me a convert to the "let's see if we can get Graham a good night's sleep" campaign.'

'That is wonderful news, sir.' Graham's eyes filled with water. 'Thank you, sir, thank you very much,' he blurted.

'Go home now, and leave the rest to us. As soon as we have some news for you, Martin will inform you.'

Martin stood up. 'Thank you, Chief. You are a bit of a softie, really. I guess I owe you another coffee?'

The chief would not let anyone else in the station speak to him like that, but he had an excellent detective in Martin and tolerated his banter.

'Get out of here before I change my mind,' he jibed.

Martin and Graham left the chief's office.

'Leave the door open,' were his final words as the two of them left.

Martin escorted Graham to the station's front door. He wished him good luck and reassured him again that they would do all they could to get the loot released for him.

'I will spend a couple more days here before I return to Portsmouth. There will be some arrangements to be made with Pam on how we will keep in contact with each other. I don't want her being snapped up by some silver-tongued detective.'

'Not much chance of that, Graham. Don't worry, I will keep an eye on her for you. Anyway, I am happily married,' Martin said, pulling his leg.

'Thanks, Martin. I have gained a lot of respect for you in the last week, and I apologise for any grief I have given you.'

'Believe me, Graham, I have never had such an unusual and interesting case in my whole ten years as a detective. Now hop it before you have me welling up.'

Graham turned around and walked away, and Martin headed to his office with his faith in humanity fully restored.

The rest of the week Graham spent loafing around. It saddened him that he had to leave Pam behind, but in his heart he knew he had to go and try to pick up the pieces of his normally orderly life that had been turned upside down by his dreams. Friday night was their last night together. They talked and planned how they would keep in touch, and he said he would phone on the weekends. They swapped birthday dates. She said she had some holiday time due and could book into a hotel in Portsmouth.

'Oh no, you won't. You will spend it with me and Mum,' he ordered. 'One final thing, Don't go finding another boyfriend.' He said this jokingly.

'Don't you find another girlfriend either. If you do, it will break my heart.'

They stayed talking until the early hours. When they finally parted, they both felt they were leaving behind all their happiness. The following morning, he packed his case, checked out of the hotel, and headed back home. Driving back, he asked himself, 'Is this all part of a master plan? Is this my destiny? Was it all planned over one hundred years ago? Surely not—don't be so stupid.'

CHAPTER NINE

The following Monday, Professor Irvin was busy in his office trying to find a common denominator out of all the data that his team had submitted from the previous week's work when the phone rang. 'Graham, how are you, my boy?'

'I am back in town now and need to get my life back again. I would like to speak to you if possible, Professor.'

'Of course, my boy. Come in this afternoon. You can tell me all about it. In truth, I can't wait to hear it all.'

'Thanks, Professor, I'll see you at about 3 p.m.'

'Mother, have you seen my pass to get into the laboratory?'

'All of your stuff you left scattered around I picked up and put it all in the bottom drawer of your dressing table, Graham.'

'Thanks, Mother. I guess I have treated you quite badly these last few weeks. Can I apologise now? But if you knew the torment and stress that I have been under, I am sure you would forgive me.'

'Yes, Graham, you haven't really explained yourself to me yet. Perhaps we can sit down together tonight and you can enlighten me?'

'I would like that, Mother. God only knows you deserve an explanation.'

At 3 p.m., Graham found himself knocking on the professor's door. The door opened.

'Graham, my boy, come in.' The professor grabbed Graham's hand and nearly shook his arm off. 'Welcome back, my boy. Now please sit down and tell me all about it?'

Graham recited his events with the same attention to detail that so impressed Martin.

'I said Annie Philpot had more secrets to reveal, didn't I?' said the professor, proud of his contribution.

'It was exactly that, Professor, that unlocked the clue to the whereabouts of the loot.'

'But one thing puzzles me—why on earth didn't you report your suspicions to the police? You could have saved yourself a lot of grief.'

'I did, but they treated me as a joke. When I told them I had dreamt it, they literally pushed me out of the station. That is when I decided to do it alone. I would have got away with it if I hadn't been spotted digging up poor Annie's grave at three in the morning.'

'What about the dreams—have they gone yet?'

'No, and I don't think they will until I hand over the loot to its rightful owner, the Goldsteins. That is what I am banking on.'

'How long will that take?'

'Everyone at Hamwell police station is working to get it released early, including the chiefs, so I am hoping it will be sooner rather than later. One good thing that has come out of all this is I have fallen in love.'

'Who is she? Anyone I know?'

'Don't laugh, but she is the police constable who was interviewing me.'

'Well, I never, Graham. You really do take the biscuit. Now, my boy, for the million-dollar question—do you feel you are ready to return to the team?'

'I would love to, sir, but if you feel I am struggling, you must drop me again, but I will do my utmost to leave my personal problems at home.'

'That is what I wanted to hear, Graham,'

'When shall I start, sir?'

'Well, there is no time like the present. How about tomorrow?'

'Fantastic, sir. When I get my life back on an even keel, I want to research thought transference from the dead to the living. I think the subject holds great possibilities.'

'That sounds really exciting, Graham. How do you intend to address the subject?'

'I thought I might advertise in the papers for people that have had similar experiences to mine to come and share them with me, and if I felt they were worth investigating, then I would investigate their past and try to find the catalyst that has triggered their experience because I am totally convinced that I have inherited a dead person's thoughts, so if it can happen to me, then why not others?'

'I think you have inherited a fantastic subject to study, and I look forward to seeing the outcome.'

'You will be the first to read it, sir. I suppose I had better be off now. I have got work tomorrow. Wow, you don't know how good that felt, saying that.' He left the professor with a new spring in his step, feeling his troubles would soon be behind him. He made his way home, thinking once he had recited his adventure to his mother, he could close his mind to the subject until he was contacted by Hamwell police station. That night, he sat down with his mother and related the whole story to her. After he had finished, his mother looked physically shaken.

'So if I hadn't encouraged you to visit your grandmother, you would have been none the wiser. It seems we had a seedy character as a distant relative, doesn't it, Graham?'

'Yes, we did, Mother, but then again, if I had not accompanied you, Arthur Tidwell might have been banging away in my head every night until he drove me crazy, and that is really frightening.'

'And who, young man, is this Pam that you keep going on about?'

'She is the most beautiful girl in the world and has been a pillar of strength this last few weeks. She believed me from the outset. She has a holiday coming shortly, and if you don't mind, I was going to ask her to come and stay with us.'

'Of course. It will give me something to look forward to. I do hope I find her as nice as you have described her. We must take her to meet Gran.'

'Wow, hold your horses, Mother. You might not like her.'

'Of course I will, dear.' She was already thinking about what to wear at the wedding.

'I think I will have an early night, Mother. It has been a tiring day.'

'Okay, son, and if that nasty Arthur Tidwell pays you a visit, you tell him he will have me to answer to.'

'Sure thing, Mother. That should scare him off. Good night.' He flopped himself down on his bed and picked up his phone and rang Pam. He told her he was starting back at work. He also told her that he had spoken to his mother about her and was going to invite her to stay during her holidays.

'How did she react, Graham?' Pam enquired.

'She was thrilled. I think she was beginning to think I was going to stay a bachelor all my life.'

'That sounds like a proposal, Graham.'

'Does it? Well, I suppose I had better buy a ring.'

'Ahhh, do you mean it, darling?'

'Yes, sweetheart, I mean it.' He could hear her sobbing on the other end of the phone. 'Stop crying, Pam. I am not that bad to live with.'

'You know I love you, Graham?'

'I love you too, Pam. Now go to sleep, and I will phone you at the same time tomorrow.' He lay back on his bed and said to himself, 'What happened there? I only rang to say hello, now I am engaged to be married. Life is sure going at a gallop.' He thought, *I hope it is going as well in Hamwell.*

Back in Hamwell, the chief superintendent had just walked into the clubhouse of his local golf club. He was feeling quite pleased with himself. He had posted an 85, and he hadn't done that for quite a while. A voice calling his name made him turn around. 'Ronald, you old devil, how are you?' It was the crown prosecuting officer, Cecil Smythe.

'Cecil, you old rascal, long time, no see. Have you had a good round?'

'No, I went around like a man with no eyes, and you?'

'I shot an 85—that's the best round I have had for a long time.'

'What are you playing off of now?'

'21.'

'21, let me see—85 taken off of 21 gives you a net 64. You, my man, need your handicap looked at.'

'What's your poison, Ronald?'

'Whisky and soda please, Cecil. I am glad I have seen you, there is something I would like your opinion on.'

They both sat down, and Ronald began to tell him of the case of Graham Peters, how everything this young man had claimed was the truth and had been checked and double-checked and they couldn't find one single discrepancy in his statement—how his dreams led him to the loot. Forensics checked out the grave and concluded it had not been opened since 1911 when the occupant was buried. What he was claiming was that his great-great-grandfather was the murderer and he had inherited his thought DNA, and it was the guilt of his dead relative that he was

Do You Believe in Life After Death?

experiencing, and he was convinced that the guilt would not go until he had righted the wrong and returned the stolen property to its rightful owner.

'And does he know who the rightful owner is?' asked Cecil.

'Oh yes, he has done all his homework,'

'And do you believe him, Ronald?'

'It goes against all common sense, but yes, I do.'

'And what do you want me to do?'

'I want you to help me get permission to get the stolen property released so he can return it to the Goldsteins. There is one plus in this case—he has solved a case of murder and robbery that has been lying in our files since 1911.'

'Okay, Ronald, send me over the case history, and I will give it my full attention. Now don't let's ruin a day's golf by talking shop.'

'Thanks, Cecil. My round, I think.'

Half an hour had passed, and Ronald would normally have put his clubs in his locker and left, but with just two pairings to come in and him sitting on top of the leader board, he held back to see if he had won. Cecil bought another round of drinks and was waiting to see the outcome of the competition as well. The final pairings came into the clubhouse. Ronald overheard comments like 'I was rubbish' and 'I think I will invest in some new clubs.' Tom Poole, who played off a handicap of 8, said he had a great round, then looked up at the leader board and uttered, 'But not that great.' After the final pairing posted their score, Ronald breathed a sigh of relief. The club captain announced the winner.

'The winner of this month's medal is Ron Hawkins.' Everyone clapped, and Ronald could hear friendly banter. 'He's a bandit' and 'Cut his handicap' and 'Give the rest of us a chance.' He took it all in good spirit then gave a little speech on how Lady Luck had played the major part in the days success, then finished his drink with Cecil and rang for a taxi to take him home. The following morning, he called Martin into his office.

'Martin, I want you to gather up all the evidence we have on Peter's case—that includes the outstanding case history we have on the murder of Mr Goldstein—and send it to the crown prosecution service for the attention of Cecil Smythe. I spoke to him yesterday, and if he agrees with our findings, he will try and get the proceeds of the robbery fast-tracked for release.'

'That is good news, sir, I was thinking to myself, in a job that deals every day in personal grief and misery, it is quite refreshing to do something good for society. I think Graham Peters can teach us all a lesson.'

'You're right, Martin. He certainly is a remarkable young man.'

Martin left the chief's office, remembering to leave the door open. He had the feeling that things were finally gaining momentum.

CHAPTER TEN

The next three months were difficult for Graham. Arthur Tidwell was extremely active in his dreams, and it was beginning to show in his face. His eyes were looking black with tiredness, and the strain had made him lose a stone in weight. He was trying his hardest to hold it all together at the laboratory. Professor Irvin had noticed that he was struggling but kept himself at a respectable distance so as not to worry him even further. He knew that dropping him from the team for a second time would have a devastating effect on his young prodigy's morale.

It was common knowledge now back in Hamwell that Pam Turner and Graham Peters were an item. Martin, in particular, was delighted for them both. It was because she was looking rather gloomy one day that he asked if everything was all right between her and Graham. He had hardly finished asking her when the waterworks started.

'I'm so worried about him,' she sobbed. 'He isn't handling it at all well. His eyes are black with tiredness, and he seems to have lost all his lust for life. Just how long is it going to take for him to get peace of mind?'

'Come with me, Pam,' he said. 'We will go and see the chief super together. He might have some news for you.'

'Thank you, sir,' she said, wiping the tears from her eyes.

'Go and get yourself a cup of tea whilst I see if he is available.' He headed straight to the chief's office. The door was open as usual. 'Have you got a moment, Chief?'

'What is it, Martin?'

'I have someone who wants a word with you.'

'Okay, bring him in.'

'It's a lady, sir. I will go and get her. I have left her waiting in the canteen.' He returned two minutes later with Pam.

'WPC Turner, isn't it? What can I do for you?'

Martin stepped in. 'I don't know if you are aware, sir, but WPC Turner and Graham Peters are an item.'

'There is not much that goes on in this station that I don't know about, so what is your point?'

'It is Graham, sir,' blurted Pam. 'He is making himself ill. His dreams are getting worse. He is losing weight, and I am very concerned for him. I am frightened he might go and do something silly. Please help him, sir.' She was now crying uncontrollably.

'Believe me, Miss Turner, we are doing our best, but these things do take time. Now pull yourself together and come and see me tomorrow afternoon, and I might have a bit more information for you.'

'Thank you, sir,' she sniffed through her handkerchief.

Martin escorted her out of the chief's office and ordered her to go to the ladies to regain her composure, then he doubled back to the chief's office.

'Is there nothing we can do, Chief, to speed up the release of the loot? I think we are all in agreement that it does, indeed, belong to the Goldsteins.'

'Believe me, Martin, from my point of view, I feel I have acted promptly, but I agree with you— the wheels of progress do seem to have grinded to a halt. I have got a good mind to just release it here and now, Martin, but I asked Cecil Smythe of the Crown Prosecution office to advise me of what action to take. I was hoping he would have contacted me by now. Come back tomorrow with WPC Turner, and I might have some news for her.'

As soon as Martin had left his office, the chief phoned Cecil Smythe. His secretary answered the phone.

'I am afraid he is in court today,' she said. 'Can I take a message?'

'Would you ask him to ring Ronald Hawkins when he gets in, please?'

'Certainly, sir, does he have your phone number?'

'Yes, he does. Could you add that it is urgent?'

Ronald put the phone down and began to consider his options. If the news went against an early release, should he play it safe and wait for permission to be granted? If he did that, who knows what Graham would do if it became too much for him to bear? Or should he just go ahead and to hell with the consequences, doing what Graham did when he tried to do the right thing, but had the misfortune of telling his story to the baboon, and that was to do it alone and worry about it later? His thoughts went to Pam, a young girl with her whole life ahead of her, a young girl deeply in love with her boyfriend who might do something stupid if his torment continued. He recalled his own courtship and wondered how he would have felt if something had happened to the love of his life and there was somebody out there who could have prevented it. He had come to a decision. He would not risk having something like that hanging over him for the rest of his life. 'I will act tomorrow,' he told himself.

The following morning, he received the call he was waiting for.

'Ronald, Cecil here, you wanted me?'

'Cecil, have you read that case that I sent you?'

'Yes, I have. Fascinating. I have passed it around the practice for separate opinions, and we have come up with a couple of theories on how he managed it, but they both fell apart when we discussed it as a team. The only conclusion that held any credibility was that he did indeed dream it, and if he did, then perhaps his dead relative did pass over his thoughts in his DNA.'

'The reason I asked you to ring today is I am in a dilemma as what to do. This is how it is—one of my WPCs has fallen in love with Mr Peters, and she came to see me yesterday in a flood of tears. She told me she was extremely concerned for her boyfriend's health. His dreams are getting worse, and his health is deteriorating. He is absolutely certain the dreams will only subside when he returns the loot to its rightful owner. What I need from you is your approval.'

'The law does allow the return of stolen goods to its owner, but of course, the owner must prove that it is their property. In this particular case, the owner is dead. However, your intrepid explorer has proved beyond little doubt that the property does indeed belong to the Goldstein family.'

'What are you saying, Cecil?'

'What I am saying, Ronald, is whatever you decide, I am sure you will make the right decision. You will not hear any objections from this department.'

'Thanks, Cecil. I owe you a drink. By the way, I've had my handicap cut by two strokes.'

'About time,' laughed Cecil.

CHAPTER ELEVEN

Friday afternoon, Pam and Martin made their way to the chief's office. She knew he was going to talk about Graham but had a terrible feeling it was going to be bad news. His office door was wide open as usual, and the chief beckoned them both in.

'Close the door please, Martin,' he said in a very formal voice that Martin was unfamiliar with, which made him also think bad news was on its way.

'I have taken advice on what we were talking about yesterday and have been advised that there is no reason why the proceeds of the robbery cannot be returned to the descendants of the family of the deceased Mr Goldstein.'

'Oh, thank you, sir, thank you, thank you, thank you! I can't wait to tell Graham!' And yet another 'Thank you, sir! You have made me so happy!' she sang.

'Hold on, young lady. It's not quite that easy. We have to plan a date and make sure all participants are available and where the handing over should take place. What I thought was that we use the briefing room. It is the only room in this station that is suitable for such an event. What do you think, Martin?'

'That should do adequately, sir.'

'As you are familiar with all the people who will be involved in the returning of the goods, Martin, I will leave you to do the arranging.'

'Very good, Chief.'

'Don't tell the Goldsteins what is going on until the day, just in case we run into a snag and we have to cancel it. How long do you think you will need to arrange it?'

'No more than a week, sir.'

'Good, then let's say not next Tuesday but the Tuesday after, and make it for 2 p.m.'

'It's as good as done, Chief.'

'Let's hope this cures your young man's nightmares, WPC Turner.'

Pam physically shuddered at the thought that it might not.

'That is it for now. Any questions?' said the chief.

'No, sir.'

'Good. Leave the door open on the way out.'

They walked away from his office. Martin was already working out who to get in touch with. 'I am sure I can rely on you to inform Graham of our arrangements, Pam?'

'I will tell him tonight, sir. He could do with a bit of good news.' Her shift finished at five, and she arrived home at 5.20 p.m. and immediately phoned Graham's house. His mother answered.

'Hello, Mrs Peters, it's Pam.'

'Hello, Pam, I am afraid he is not in yet.'

'How is he bearing up, Mrs Peters?'

'Not good, Pam.'

'Well, Mrs Peters, I have some wonderful news for him. The chief superintendent has agreed to release the stolen goods for Graham to hand back to the Goldsteins.'

'That is marvellous, Pam. When?'

'Tuesday week at 2 p.m. at Hamwell police station.'

'When he comes in, I will tell him you phoned, and I will convey the good news to him, Pam, and you will ring him later tonight, won't you?'

'You try and stop me.'

'Why don't you come and stay with us for the weekend, Pam? We both would be so happy to see you, and Graham could certainly do with something to take his mind off his problems, and I can't think of a better distraction than you.'

'I would love to. I will see you Saturday morning. Don't tell him—we will surprise him.'

'Wonderful, Pam. I will see you then. Don't forget to phone him tonight.'

'Of course not. Goodbye.'

Graham arrived home at 6.15 p.m. He entered the lounge and flopped down on a chair. It was Friday, and he had just about managed to struggle through another week. 'I can't take much more of this,' he told his mother.

'Yes, you can, dear. I've made you a nice cup of coffee. Now relax and drink it. I have some news for you.'

'It will have to be something special to cheer me up.'

'Oh, it is, Graham. Pam phoned less than an hour ago, and she said they are going to release the stolen goods for you to hand back to the family that it was stolen from.'

'You're not just saying that, Mother, just to cheer me up, are you?'

'Of course not, dear.'

'When will they release it?' he asked.

'It will take place Tuesday week at 2 p.m. at Hamwell police station.'

'Mother, that is wonderful. Let me see—eight, nine, ten, eleven days' time. Did you hear that, Arthur Tidwell? You will soon be able to rest in peace.'

'That is more like my boy,' she said. 'Are you feeling hungry? I have made a nice hot stew for you.'

'Thanks, Mother. I will try a little.'

Mrs Peters returned to the kitchen, relieved to see her son had regained a little of his fighting spirit.

He ate his dinner. It was the first time in a long while that he looked at food and actually had the desire to eat it. He retired to his bedroom after his dinner and lay on his bed, hoping Pam would phone. His bedside clock read 8 p.m., the time she normally rang. She didn't disappoint him.

'Hello, darling,' she said. 'Has your mother given you the news?'

'Yes, she has. Isn't it fantastic? But how did you get to hear about it?'

'I told Martin how worried I was about you, and he suggested we go to see the chief super, so that's what we did. I'm afraid I had a few tears, but my point must have got across because the next day, he called us both back to his office and told us the good news. He gave Martin the task of arranging it, so next week, he will contact all the people who need to be there so that there are no hiccups on the day.'

'Pamela Turner, you are bloody marvellous, and I can't tell you how much I love you. When we tell our children about all of this, they will never believe us.'

'You must be feeling better to be talking about having children, Graham, but I do suggest we get married first.'

'Of course, darling, but once this is over, you had better start looking for a wedding dress.'

'I have news for you, babe. I already am.'

Graham laughed, 'What a girl you are, Miss Turner. I don't deserve you.'

Saturday morning, Graham awoke from a particularly vivid dream. Arthur had made his usual appearance, conveying all the guilt and sorrow he could muster to ruin a good night's sleep. After he had eaten his breakfast, two slices of toast and a cup of strong coffee, he decided to take a walk. He headed for the local park. The early morning was a good time for a stroll in the park. Listening to the birds singing gave him peace of mind and a feeling that life wasn't too bad after all. He sat on a bench that was placed to observe the duck pond. *I wonder if ducks dream?* he thought. 'Listen to me,' he said to himself. 'You can't even go for a walk without thinking about those dreams.' a horrible thought crossed his mind and sent him into a cold sweat; it was the same thought that had made Pam shudder in horror. 'Suppose once I have handed the stolen goods back, I still have the dreams. What do I do then?' He took a deep breath. 'Take those negative thoughts out of your mind, and stay positive. Only ten days to go. Should I visit the Goldsteins and tell them the whole story beforehand? What if he blames me for what my relative did? Say he doesn't want the gold?' This stroll in the park was turning into a nightmare, he thought. He decided to head back home, as it seemed there was nowhere he could gain peace of mind. He turned into his road when the sound of a car horn made him look around. What a sight for sore eyes. Pam had pulled up alongside him, and her beautiful smile lifted his spirits instantly. 'Jump in, handsome,' she joked.

'I wasn't expecting to see you this weekend,' he said, putting his head through the open window and giving her a welcoming kiss.

'Your mum suggested I come and stay for the weekend, but she didn't tell you because she wanted it to be a surprise. I hope you don't mind.'

'Hope I don't mind? Are you kidding? I am delighted,' he said, giving her a hug. 'Let us go and see Mother, and you can tell us all the news.'

When they arrived home, Graham's mother came to the door to greet them.

'Pam, what a surprise. How lovely to see you.' She was trying to make out that she knew nothing about her coming. 'Please come in.'

Graham gave Pam a sly glance but said nothing. He escorted Pam to the lounge, and his mother headed for the kitchen to make the coffee.

'You must bring me up to speed with what is happening back at Hamwell, Pam. Is it still on for Tuesday week?' he pressed.

'Yes, it is, dear, they are going to do the handover in the briefing room.'

'I must come up to Hamwell. I feel I should inform Jeff Goldstein about what is happening,' he said.

'No, you must not do that. The chief has told Martin not to tell them what is happening until the last day.'

'Why not, Pam?'

'If there should be a last-minute hitch, then they would be none the wiser.'

'Let's hope they don't decide to go on holiday next week.'

'I will mention that possibility to Martin when I get back, but don't worry, Graham, I will make sure everything goes according to plan.'

Graham's mother returned with a tray of coffee. 'There we are, you two lovebirds,' she said in a way that would embarrass the most insensitive of sons.

'Thank you, Mrs Peters, I need this. It was a long drive from London.'

'I thought we might go shopping this afternoon, Pam,' said Graham.

'Graham, what are you thinking about? That is the last thing she wants to do after a long drive,' argued his mother.

'Mother, you wouldn't say that if you knew what we were shopping for.'

'What are we shopping for, Graham?' Pam enquired.

'An engagement ring, of course, what else would we go shopping for?'

Pam leapt up from her chair and held Mrs Peters's hands, and they both jumped around the room in sheer delight.

'I just knew you two were made for each other,' said his mother. A little tear came in her eye. 'I wish your father was still alive, Graham. He would be so proud now, and he would have loved Pam.'

'That is such a lovely thing to say, Mrs Peters. I feel I am part of the family already,' Pam replied.

'We will leave shortly, Mother. Don't bother making dinner. We will eat out.'

'Why don't you come too, Mrs Peters? You can help me choose the ring,' suggested Pam.

'Are you sure? Wouldn't you two rather be alone?'

'I would love you to come,' Pam reassured her.

'Yes, come with us, Mother. It will be great fun,' said Graham.

'Okay, I will, but I will pay for lunch.'

'You will get no argument from me, Mother.'

They had a wonderful afternoon out. Pam and Graham's mother were arm in arm all afternoon, going from shop to shop. Graham stood back and let the two of them bond. He knew that this girl was, without question, going to be the love of his life. After visiting every jeweller's in Portsmouth, she decided the one she really liked was in the first shop they had looked at.

'Okay, ladies,' he said. 'Let's eat first, then we will go back and buy it.'

The weekend seemed to fly by, and it wasn't long before they were saying their goodbyes to Pam.

'Goodbye, darling. Goodbye, Mrs Peters. I have had a wonderful weekend. I don't want to go back, and I really enjoyed our little shopping trip.'

'So did I, Pam. I have a feeling it won't be our last shopping trip together.' She was already thinking of Pam as the daughter she longed for but never had. She held her hand, looking down at her ring, saying how beautiful it looked on her finger, then told her to drive carefully, then she watched her drive away. They both stood at the front door and waved goodbye until Pam had disappeared around the corner. It felt like some of their joy had left them.

CHAPTER TWELVE

The next week dragged by for Graham, but for Martin, it flew by. Trying to do his normal detective duties and organising the following Tuesday's handover of the stolen goods wasn't easy. He heeded Pam's advice regarding the availability of the Goldsteins and rang Len, asking him if he could help out by visiting them and spinning them some story that would make sure they were available for Tuesday afternoon. Len agreed and visited the Goldsteins on that Friday morning. He gave them his card and told them he had some information that could possibly be to their advantage. He could not say more at that present moment in time, but if they could make themselves available the following Tuesday, he would explain it then. 'Do you have a car, Mr Goldstein?' he asked. He had already noticed there was no sign of one on the road outside.

'No, I haven't,' said Jeff. 'I have a bike though.'

'Not to worry, I will pick you up at 1 p.m.—if that is agreeable with you?'

'Well yes,' said Jeff, totally bewildered by it all. 'Shall I bring my wife?'

'Of course, Mr Goldstein.'

'What about the twins?'

'Why not?' said Len. 'The more, the merrier.'

He picked up his briefcase, thanked them for their time, and left.

'What was that all about?' said Mary.

'I haven't got the foggiest,' said Jeff. 'It's probably a long-lost relative has died and left me his dirty washing.'

Mary laughed and shoved him, sending him flying on to the settee. 'You are a fool, Jeff,' she said affectionately.

Tuesday morning finally came. Martin spent his time organising the briefing room. Graham and his mother arrived at midday. Pam asked Sergeant Edward for the afternoon off. Knowing her circumstances, he gladly agreed. Len had picked up the Goldsteins. To his relief, Mary had made an arrangement for her mother to babysit for the afternoon. Chief Superintendent Hawkins sat in his office when Cecil Smythe walked in. 'What on earth are you doing here, Cecil? Please don't tell me you have found a reason we can't go ahead.'

'Don't panic, Ronald. It's just a matter of curiosity killing the cat. I want to see this young man myself.'

'Why didn't you say? I would have laid on some lunch.'

Len entered the police station with the Goldsteins. Jeff was getting decidedly nervous. 'Hold on a minute, I thought you said we were going to your office,' he complained. His dislike of police stations was quite evident, and he was already feeling very unsettled.

Martin had finished in the briefing room and was making his way back to his office when he spotted Len and the Goldsteins. 'Perfect timing, Len. Please come into my office, Mr and Mrs Goldstein.'

They entered sheepishly into his office, like two naughty children being taken to see the headmaster.

'Please take a seat, Mr and Mrs Goldstein. Who is looking after the children?' Martin enquired, hoping they were not going to say 'Nobody'.

'My mother is,' said Mary.

'Excellent. Have you any idea why you are here?' asked Martin.

'This man here,' said Jeff, pointing at Len, 'he said it is about something to our advantage. Other than that, we have no idea.'

'Well, where shall I start?' said Martin, lying back in his chair and resting both hands at the back of his head.

'It all started with a man having some disturbing dreams, three names always cropping up in the dreams. Perhaps it would be more accurate to call them nightmares. One of the names was Goldstein, and the other two were Annie Philpot and Arthur Tidwell. He couldn't understand, for the life of him, why the same names kept appearing night after night. It was only when he visited his grandmother and she asked him why he was looking so pale and drawn that he told her about one of the names that he kept dreaming about. She had no idea who Goldstein or Annie Philpot was, but Arthur Tidwell, she said, was the name of his great-great-grandfather. He asked her if she knew anything about him. She told him that he had committed suicide in 1913. He had died riddled with guilt and remorse about something he had done but had never divulged to a living soul, not even his wife, but she suspected he had done something really bad. I am sorry. Where are my manners? Would you like a tea or coffee?'

'No thanks,' said Jeff. 'The sooner I am out of here, the better.'

'I would like a cup of tea, please,' said Mary, much to Jeff's annoyance.

'Well, if you're going to have one, so will I,' he said reluctantly.

'Len, how about you?'

'Yes, please. You carry on, Martin. I will get the drinks.'

'He even left his wife a suicide note stating how sorry he was. When this young man asked his gran where he lived, she told him here, in Hamwell. He decided he wanted to know more about this person who was interrupting his dreams every night. He came to Hamwell to try to learn more. The first thing he did was to visit the local cemetery to find out where his relative was buried. He never found his grave, but much to his amazement, he stumbled across the grave of Annie Philpot. He was now beginning to feel there was more to these dreams than meets the eye. In his dreams, Annie Philpot always appeared in a coffin.'

Len walked in with the drinks. He put the tray on the desk and told them to help themselves to milk and sugar.

Martin continued, 'The thing was, now, to find out who, if anybody, was Goldstein. It was sheer luck that he decided to pop into the Long Boat public house for a drink. When on the way out, he happened to look at some old photographs that showed Broad Street in years gone by. There, staring him right in the face, was a picture of your great-great-grandfather's jewellers.'

'Blimey,' said Mary, looking around at Jeff.

'His next step was to see if there were any relatives of Mr Goldstein who were still living. He looked in the phone book—there were four. He rang them all and asked if they were relatives of the Goldstein that owned the jewellers on Broad Street. One person said they were, and that person, Mr Goldstein, was—as I expect you realise by now—you.'

'You're talking about Graham Peters, aren't you?' said Mary, beating her husband to the conclusion by a country mile.

'What a dirty rat,' said Jeff.

'Please let me finish before you start judging him,' said Martin in Graham's defence. 'To continue, I haven't told you yet, but Graham Peters is a biological scientist, whose field of work is trying to find cures for various forms of cancers, and he is much respected within his profession. Have either of you heard of the term *déjà vu*?'

'Yes, I have,' said Mary.

'Do you know what it means?' asked Martin.

Do You Believe in Life After Death?

'Not really,' she said.

'It means having a feeling that you have been somewhere before, even though you haven't, or maybe something has happened to you before, but you don't know what or where. Anyway, that is the feeling Graham Peters had when he was on Broad Street. Halfway down Broad Street, there is an alleyway—it is called the Mews. It seemed to give off some strong feelings when he entered it. He looked over the wall into a courtyard. The feelings he experienced were getting stronger and stronger. He walked to the front of the building—you might know it as Smithers and Sons solicitors. He went in and asked Mr Smithers what the building had been at the beginning of the twentieth century. He was told it was an undertaker's. He now had all the pieces of the puzzle to make an educated guess as to what was happening. He was almost certain that what he was experiencing was the DNA of his distant relative that he had inherited, contacting him through his dreams, asking him to put right a wrong that he had committed in 1911, and that was robbing and murdering your great-great-grandfather. You told Graham yourself that the police chased him but lost him along Broad Street, so on that information, he worked out that he had hopped over the undertaker's wall and lain low until the coast was clear. Not wanting to be discovered with the loot, he hid it in Annie Philpot's coffin, which Graham thought would account for the image of Annie always appearing in a coffin in his dreams. Certain of his diagnosis, he went to his local police station and asked them for their help. When they asked him where he came by the information, well, you can imagine their response when he said he dreamt it. They threw him out by his pants.'

Len interrupted, pointing to his watch. 'It's 1.45, Martin.'

'Thanks, Len. I am nearly finished. Graham was desperate to get rid of these horrible dreams, and so he made up his mind that he would do it alone. He would go to Hamwell cemetery in the middle of the night and dig up the grave of Annie Philpot,

101

retrieve the loot, and return it to its rightful owner. That is you, Mr Goldstein.'

'Well I can assure you we haven't got it,' Jeff said, as though he were being accused.

'I know you haven't, Mr Goldstein. That is where we got involved. You see, you just might have had it if Graham hadn't been spotted digging up the grave by a law-abiding citizen who promptly phoned the police. We arrested him while he was still in the grave holding the sack of stolen goods. He related the story that we just told you and challenged us to find fault with his alibi. I checked out every last word of the explanation that he gave for his actions and came to the conclusion that he was telling the truth. We will take you to him now, where he is waiting to hand over to you the proceeds of the robbery and ask your forgiveness. Please be man enough to accept it. One other thing—we have had the stolen goods valued, and thanks to Graham, you will be wealthier to the tune of £250,000.'

'Did you hear that, Mary—£250,000? We are rich!'

'Yes, Jeff, I heard,' she replied, but she was feeling too sorry for Graham to get excited about their stroke of good fortune.

Martin rose from his chair. 'Right, let's do it.' He gave Len a sly glance as if to say, 'Will this new wealth do them any good in the long run? I doubt it.'

They walked into the briefing room, where everyone was waiting. Graham sat centre stage with the stolen goods laid out on three large trays, and it looked amazingly clean and shiny considering how long it had been buried. Jeff couldn't take his eyes off it; however, Mary went straight to Graham, noticing how much he had deteriorated since the last time they had met, and said, 'You dear brave man. I do hope you soon find peace.'

'Thanks, Mary. How are the twins?'

'They're fine, Graham.' She backed away, looking at all those present. Other than Len and Martin, there was no one she recognised.

The chief super stood in one corner with Cecil Smythe. Mrs Peters and Pam stood in the opposite corner. Pam had her arm around Mrs Peters's arm for comfort.

Martin took the stage. 'Graham, I have explained to Mr and Mrs Goldstein how we have arrived at this moment in time. First I would like to thank all of the people who have helped us. I would like to thank Len Brown Graham's solicitor, who to my shame questioned what to me looked like a straightforward case. Next, I would like to thank Chief Superintendent Hawkins for believing in me and for all the work he has done behind the scenes to achieve a quick release of the stolen goods. And last but not least, WPC Pam Turner, who believed in Graham from the outset, so much so she is going to marry him.' Pam could feel her face going red. 'Sorry, Pam, I hope I haven't embarrassed you. Anyway, enough from me, Graham. It's over to you.'

'Thank you, Martin, for briefing Jeff and Mary and for not writing me off as a nut case.'

'Who told you that?' joked Martin, trying to take a little of the tension out of the occasion.

'Mary, Jeff, I must first apologise for entering your lives on a lie. I was still gathering facts about what my great-great-grandfather did, and at that particular time, I was still not sure. I am sure now and would like to take this opportunity to right his wrong.'

Pam took out her mobile phone and started to film Graham's speech.

'I would like to hand back the stolen goods to you now, and . . . and . . .' There was a pause of about five seconds that seemed like a lifetime, then his face drained of colour, then he spoke, but it was not Graham's voice. It was a voice totally alien to his own. It sounded like a voice of an older man, a man in mental pain, with a more common accent than Graham's. 'I am sorry. I didn't mean to kill you,' it said. Everyone stood in amazement as Graham crumpled to the floor unconscious. About three minutes passed before he began to gain consciousness. He could hear Pam saying, 'Graham, wake up.' Somebody else was saying, 'Loosen his collar and give him some air.' They pulled him up on to a chair. 'What happened?' he uttered, still feeling groggy.

'If I'm not mistaken, Graham, you have just exorcised your demons,' said Len, totally flabbergasted by what he had just witnessed.

Mary was crying. 'Please let him be all right,' she wept.

Mrs Peters had hastily returned from getting a glass of water and was giving Graham small sips.

Cecil spoke to the chief. 'Well, Ronald, you certainly know how to put on a show. I wouldn't have missed that for all the tea in China. Come on, you can buy me a coffee.'

'Just hold on one moment, Cecil.' He walked over to Graham and asked him if he was all right, then turned to Martin.

'Well done, Martin. You handled that very professionally. But the exorcism was a turn-up for the books, wasn't it?'

'You're telling me, Chief. I don't mind telling you it frightened the life out of me.'

The chief agreed it was very unnerving. 'I am taking Cecil for a coffee. Perhaps you could join us when you are finished here?'

'I don't know how long that will be, sir, but if you're still there when I am finished, I would be glad to.'

The chief said his goodbyes to everyone then retreated with Cecil to the canteen.

Graham had fully recovered from his out-of-body experience and was feeling like a heavy load had been lifted off of his brain. His mother, Pam, and Mary were all still fussing over him, even though he kept insisting that he felt fine and that there was nothing to worry about. Jeff, in a rare moment of compassion, leaned down in front of Graham and took his hand. 'I don't know what happened there, mate, but I could see it was a painful experience for you, so let me just say on behalf of myself, my wife, and all of those

Do You Believe in Life After Death?

Goldsteins dead and gone, we accept your apology, and you can tell that to that other bloke who is living inside your head.'

'Thanks, Jeff, and you, Mary. I hope your newfound wealth will improve your lifestyle. Don't go spending it all at once.'

'That he won't be doing, I can assure you of that,' said Mary, in a light-hearted but determined voice.

Martin interrupted, 'This is an excellent time, Mr and Mrs Goldstein, to exchange gold into cash, and the price of gold is at an all-time high. One more thing—I don't advise you to go waltzing out of here with £250,000 worth of gold in your handbag.'

'Why don't you leave it in the police station under lock and key and let me negotiate the best price possible for you?' said Len. 'That way, you will have the option to take an offer now or wait for a better one.'

'What do you think Graham?' said Jeff.

'It sounds like common sense to me, Jeff.'

'Okay, we will do that. Is that all right with you, Mary?'

'If Graham says it is, then it is all right with me.' Her faith in Graham was quite touching.

'Good, that's settled then,' said Martin, eager to tie up all the loose ends.

'Are you ready to be taken home now, Mr and Mrs Goldstein?' said Len, who was, in truth, getting a little bored.

'Just one last look at the gold,' said Jeff.

'I can't wait to tell my mum,' said Mary, then they both thanked Graham again and left with Len.

'Pam, can I just borrow you for a second to help me get this gold locked away safely?'

'Of course, sir. I will be back soon, dear,' she said to Graham, squeezing his hand.

'Mrs Peters, please feel free to use the canteen. You and your son must be quite thirsty by now. I know I am,' said Martin.

105

'That would be most welcome, Officer. Come on, Graham, it's all over now,' she said, helping him off the chair.

Martin and Pam finished putting the valuables away and returned to the canteen. Pam went to sit with Graham and his mother, and Martin headed toward the Chief and Cecil.

'We have returned the goods to the safe, sir, until Len Brown tries to sell it for the Goldsteins.'

'That is marvellous,' said the chief. 'It couldn't have worked out better.'

'What do you mean, sir?' said Martin, somewhat confused.

'Well, Graham has exorcised his demons, the Goldsteins have their gold, and all that worrying that I did about whether I should let the gold be released or not doesn't matter because we still have it, so sit down and stop making the canteen look untidy.'

Martin could tell that the chief was cock-a-hoop with the outcome and felt that his role in the case hadn't done his reputation any harm either.

'I haven't introduced you yet, Martin. This is Cecil Smythe from the Crown Prosecution services, and Cecil, my star, DI Martin Penn. I don't think you two have met before.'

'I have seen you in court once or twice, Cecil, and I thought you were very impressive.'

'Why, thank you, Martin. You were quite impressive yourself today. I am in little doubt that what just happened was genuine. If it wasn't, your Mr Peters gave an Oscar-winning performance.'

'I have got to know Graham rather well over the last few months, and almost from the time I pulled him out of Annie Philpot's grave, I could tell he was no ordinary crook. His honesty shone through like a beacon, and when he explained what he thought was happening to him and with the logic that he applied to his detection skills, well, it would put the best of detectives to shame.'

'It is a shame his case didn't come to court. I would love to know what the legal profession would make of it.'

'Well, Cecil, interrupted the chief, you might get the chance later, not with this case, but Graham wants to try and find other people who have had similar experiences, and I shall offer our services if he uncovers a creditable case. He has already assisted us in solving one outstanding murder and robbery. I thought I might ask you, Martin, to help him with his enquiries, when and if he gets started.'

'I would enjoy that, sir. Can I have a boiler suit made with the words *Ghost Buster* printed on the back of it?'

All three burst into loud laughter, which made the rest of the people in the canteen turn around and stare.

'If he is up to it, Martin, I would like to meet him,' said Cecil.

'I will go and ask him.' Martin went over to where Graham was sitting. 'How are you feeling, Graham?' he said.

'I feel reborn, Martin, thanks.'

'Do you feel well enough to have a few words with the Crown Prosecution office sitting with the chief superintendent?'

'Yes, I think so.'

'Don't keep him too long, Martin. He has had a very traumatic experience.'

'Of course not, Mrs Peters,'

'Stop fussing, Mother. I feel perfectly fine now.'

Martin escorted Graham to where the chief and Cecil were sitting and introduced them to each other.

'Hello, young man,' said Cecil. 'That was some performance you just gave back there.'

'Thank you, sir, and I didn't have to rehearse it either.' He sensed that Cecil's remark was loaded with a double meaning.

'Ronald tells me that you want to do a study on your phenomenon. Is this true?' said Cecil.

'Once I get my life back into some sort of order, yes I do. I can't be the only person to have had their deceased relatives' thought DNA transferred in their genes. Who knows what secrets I might unveil?'

'Good luck with that, young man,' said Cecil, still sounding unconvinced by what his eyes had just witnessed.

'That is very kind of you,' said Graham, trying to stay dignified at what he considered was an unnecessary hint of hostility in the tone of questioning. 'It is so easy to write off what happened to me as impossible, but open your mind, look at your own children, and see how much of you is living in them. You might be surprised at how much of your DNA you have transferred to them.'

Cecil was out of his comfort zone, talking about genes and DNA, and decided to end his mini interrogation.

'If you will forgive me, gentlemen, I think I will return to the ladies,' said Graham.

'Of course,' said Ronald. 'I for one would like to say how pleased I am with the outcome and hope you can solve a few more crimes for us.' He added his support to counter Cecil's rather rude discussion. Before they left for Portsmouth, Graham and his mother treated Pam to a meal at the Ferryman hotel. There was an air of relief that seemed to infect all three of them. After discussing the events of the day, Mrs Peters made a deliberate attempt to change the subject. 'When you two get married, where do you think you will live? Have you given it any thought yet?'

'No, I haven't,' said Graham. 'I am afraid my mind has been much too preoccupied. What about you, Pam?'

'There is not much to keep me in Hamwell, and I wouldn't like to see Graham pulled away from his career. I suppose I could apply for a transfer to Portsmouth police station. I have heard they could do with some new blood down there,' she said, slipping in a little joke about the baboon. 'Then of course, I could always have a couple of children and live happily ever after.'

'I like the sound of that last option,' said Graham.

'That sounds like a wonderful idea, Pam, and you can always stay at my house until the pair of you finds your own place to live.'

'Are you sure, Mrs Peters?'

'Am I sure, you silly girl? I would love it, and while we are at it, let's have no more Mrs Peters. From now on, call me Mother.'

'Ok, I will, Mrs Pee—' She stopped herself halfway. 'Sorry, I mean Mother.'

They were all more relaxed than they had been for a long time, and it felt good.

CHAPTER THIRTEEN

Two weeks had passed, and although Graham's dreams had subsided in their intensity, he wasn't 100 per cent happy that Arthur Tidwell had left him completely. On three occasions, he had a repeating dream. There was a hand being held out, and in the palm was a gold chain and locket. The locket was in the shape of a heart roughly a half inch in diameter; etched into the heart was the word *love*. He had his suspicions as to what his latest dreams were trying to convey to him. He had an awful feeling that there was more gold to be returned to the Goldsteins but hadn't got the will to pursue it any further. He had a life to live, and nothing was going to stop him living it.

The months flew by. Professor Irvin had no need to check up on Graham's work. On the contrary, he was delighted with the commitment his young prodigy was showing towards his work, so much so that he had decided to make him team leader. He called Graham into his office to offer him his promotion. He hadn't had a good talk with him since his problems had been solved and was interested in how he was coping.

'Graham, come in. How are you?' he said it in such a way that Graham instinctively knew there was more to follow.

'Very well, thank you, Professor. Is there something wrong?'

'No, quite the contrary. I was going to offer you the position of team leader—that is, of course, if you want it. It does come with a £2,000 per annum pay raise.'

'Thank you, Professor. I accept. I can't tell you how welcome that news is,'

'Why is that, Graham?'

'I am going to get married in two months' time, so any extra cash would be most grateful.'

The professor slapped his hand on the table. 'That is marvellous, Graham. Who is it, that pretty little policewoman?'

'That's correct, sir, Pam. She was a pillar of strength during my dark days.'

'Have your dreams returned to some form of normality?'

'Almost.'

'That sounds a little worrying. I hope you are not going to leave us and resume your other career.'

'What other career is that, Professor?'

'Why, grave robbing of course.'

Graham laughed. 'Oh no, sir, those days are well and truly over. The original dream has gone, thank God. It went away when I handed over the stolen goods back to its owner's family. Exactly what I thought would happen did happen, but it has been replaced by one of far less severity, which so far I can cope with.'

'Well, are you going to tell me about it, or am I to be kept in suspense?' the professor, like all other's involved in Graham's, story was well and truly hooked, and having a small but important part in solving the mystery made him equally eager to hear the next instalment.

Graham related the dream to the professor. He told him about the hand and the gold chain and locket with the word *love* etched in it.

'What do you think it means, Graham?'

'I am not sure. I wondered, when they pulled me out of the grave and tipped all of the stolen property on to the grass, did they pick it all up, or did they leave one piece behind?'

'It is an interesting theory, but ask yourself this: if that is what happened, how did Arthur Tidwell know about it?'

'That is right, Professor, there is no way he could have known about something that happened after he had died.' They both sat deep in thought, then the professor offered up his theory. 'Just suppose he went through the stolen loot while he was hiding in the undertaker's. He spotted this chain and thought that his wife would like it, so he hides the rest of it but takes the chain home for a present for his wife. That makes sense, doesn't it, Graham?'

'It does, Professor, and if that is indeed what happened, then as far as I am concerned, it has gone forever.'

'I agree, Graham. Try and bury it in the back of your mind. You appear to have quite a lot to worry about without that.'

'That is true, Professor. Changing the subject, I wondered if you will act as my best man at my wedding?'

'I can honestly say I was not expecting that, Graham, but wouldn't you prefer someone your own age?'

'I have kind of lost touch with my old mates,' said Graham, feeling a trifle embarrassed.

'It would be an honour, my boy. I must tell the wife to start looking for a new outfit. She will be going to a wedding with the best man, and the best man will be her husband. That will tickle her pink.'

'Good, that is settled then. I will send you and your wife a formal invitation in the post.'

'Where do you intend living once you are married, here in Portsmouth or in London?'

'Pam has asked for a transfer to the Portsmouth Police station.'

'That's good,' sighed the professor. 'I thought I might lose you for a moment.'

'No chance, Professor, I am here for the long haul,' Graham reassured him.

Pam's natural parents had separated when she was a small child, and she had lost track of their whereabouts. She was adopted at the age of five and always looked upon her adopted parents as mum and dad. Rose, her adopted mother, could not have children of her own, so Pam was a gift from heaven. Ben, her adopted father, was easy-going—anything that made the ladies in his life happy was okay with him. They both took a shine to Graham and had given them their blessing. Rose, however, wasn't happy about Pam's decision to move to Portsmouth and voiced her disapproval to Ben. He took her hand. 'Rose, my dear, you worry too much,' he said in an attempt to calm her down.

'It's all right for you,' she whined. 'I am a lot closer to Pam than you are.'

'I think that's a little unfair, my dear, but don't lets argue about it. Let us both rejoice in her happiness, and let me make a suggestion.'

'What can you suggest that could possibly make it better? We are losing our daughter.'

'Look, Rose, we are both retired. We own our house outright, and I have often said that when I retire, I would like to live by the sea, so why don't we move down there? That way, you can be next to Pam and the grandchildren, and I will have the seaside. What do you think of that idea?'

'I think you are a lovely man and that it is a wonderful idea, Ben, let's do it.'

The next day, they put their plan to Pam. She thought it was a great idea, saying she also had some reservations about leaving them behind. The thought of wheeling her grandchild along the beach conjured up all kinds of happy possibilities in Rose's mind.

CHAPTER FOURTEEN

A bright, sunny Saturday morning greeted Maureen Irvin. Her social calendar was rather short of events where she had the opportunity to dress up in her finery, and being the wife of the best man certainly rated as one of those times. Although the wedding was booked for 2 p.m., she had set her alarm for 7 a.m.—she was leaving nothing to chance—and by 9 a.m., she had ironed her husband's shirt and suit and given his trousers a crease that was razor-sharp. With just breakfast to prepare, she would soon be free to devote the rest of the morning to herself. She called her husband from the foot of the stairs. 'Can you get up now, dear? Breakfast is on the table, and I hope you have not forgotten what today is.'

'Coming, Mouse,' came the reply. It was the professor's pet name for his wife, and it had originated from their courtship days when they would meet after lectures way back in their university days. They would meet on cold winter nights at the bus shelter. She would be peeking out of her scarf with just her cute little nose poking out. They would kiss, her cute little cold nose would press against his cheek, and how he loved the feeling of that mousy little snout up against his face, hence the nickname Mouse. If truth be told, she liked his little term of endearment.

Back in the Turner household, the atmosphere was a little tense.

'Stop fussing, Mother, you're making me nervous.' Mrs Turner couldn't help herself. Her daughter was getting married, and nothing less than perfection would do for her daughter's wedding. She checked her watch—her heart gave a little flutter—11 a.m. She conveyed the time to Pam. 'Three hours to go, dear. You will let me know if you need me for anything, won't you?'

'Ben!' She had now turned her attention to her husband, who was getting as far away from the hustle and bustle as possible. He had retreated to the garden, preoccupying his time by deadheading some of the wilting flowers. 'What on earth do you think you are doing?' she yelled. 'You do know our daughter will be walking up the aisle to be married in less than three hours' time. Please try and show a little interest.'

He put the scissors in his pocket, then came over to where she was standing. He took both of her hands and spoke. 'Try and relax, dear. Everything will be just fine. You're going to make yourself ill if you don't calm down, and we don't want that now, do we?' He had a way of keeping everything in perspective, and that was what she needed at this moment in time.

'You are right, dear. It is only that I don't want any hiccups. Just make sure that you are ready to leave by 1 p.m.'

'I will be. Now run along and make yourself the most beautiful mother of the bride I have ever seen.' She smiled at him and nudged him on the shoulder. 'Ben Turner,' she said, 'you really are an old charmer.' She walked away feeling quite relaxed.

Graham sat in front of his dressing table mirror. He was dressed and ready for his big day. His mother and grandmother had been fussing around him all morning. He knew that it was a big day for them also, but he needed a few moments to himself to be alone with his thoughts. Arthur Tidwell entered his thoughts. *How strange,* he thought, *that the criminal actions of a person over one hundred years ago can have such an effect on people living today and not negative effects—quite*

*the opposite, in fact—the improvement in the Goldstein's fortune, and Pam,
he thought to himself, there is no way on God's earth I would have met her.
Is our destiny already mapped out for us, or is it all simply chance?* He was
awakened by his mother's voice telling him it was time to get going
to the church.

'I am coming, Mother. Destiny or chance, in less than two
hours' time, I will be a married man,' he said to himself.

Mr and Mrs Graham Peters took centre stage at the reception
table. All the guests came over to them with their congratulations.
Martin Penn came over and thanked them for inviting him and his
wife, saying considering how they had met, he didn't know whether
he would be welcome.

'Nonsense,' said Graham. 'I am not the sort of guy who would
hold a grudge against someone who was simply doing his job.'

'And besides,' said Pam, 'you have been a true friend to both of
us in our time of need, and I am sure that I speak for my husband
and myself when I say you were at the very top of our invitation
list—cripes! that sounded strange, saying *my husband and myself.*' She
giggled a girlish laugh then leaned over to Martin and held his hand
and said, 'We both are very glad you're here.'

'I really do wish you both every happiness,' he said with
sincerity.

The sound of a booming voice commanded the attention of the
wedding guests. Everyone turned around to look at the big man
who was instructing them to take to their seats. He and his wife
proceeded to take their positions at the centre table, as best man and
his lady. The next hour was taken up with the clattering of knives,
forks, and plates and happy banter.

Somebody shouted, 'Speech!' and the professor duly obliged.
Off came his jacket, revealing his favourite Union Jack braces.
There was an air about him that commanded attention; this was his
theatre, and he was not going to let his young prodigy and friend
down. A short pause, followed by the puffing out of his chest and

a twanging of his braces, and he was flowing. First, telling his audience of the work that they did and how Graham had come to him with his dream problem and how he had fathomed out the meaning of them and how he attempted to tackle the problem, resulting in a scrape with the law, and when being interviewed by Martin and his rather beautiful sidekick, 'I won't mention her name in case she gets embarrassed,' he joked. Pam's face went scarlet. He continued, 'Now I know what you are all thinking. What a strange way to get a girlfriend! But that is Graham for you—full of surprises.' He prattled on for a good twenty minutes before finally winding up. 'Well, ladies and gentlemen, that is enough from me, so let us raise our glasses and wish the newlyweds all the happiness in the world. Ladies and gentlemen, I give you Mr and Mrs Graham Peters. Now let me hand you over to the man himself, so once again, ladies and gentlemen, I give you the groom, Mr Graham Peters.'

Graham rose to his feet. 'Well, how do I follow that?' he said rather nervously. He thanked the professor for his colourful speech then proceeded to thank everyone for coming, with special thanks to all those who worked behind the scenes to make it all run smoothly. 'I won't name everyone, otherwise we will be here all night, but you know who you are, and Pam and I thank you sincerely.' He wound up his speech by thanking his new wife for choosing him to fall in love with and making him the luckiest man on earth. A big *ah* was heard from the guests. 'Ladies and gentlemen, if you have finished your meal, please retire to the big room, where there will be music and dancing.'

The guests retired to the big room in dribs and drabs, settling down into their own family groups, and that is how they stayed all evening, reminiscing on times long since passed. The three young children present were having a whale of a time, using the big room as a playground. They had taken their shoes off and were using the highly polished floor as a skating rink. Eight p.m. and the newly married couple had changed into something more casual, They circled the room to say their goodbyes before they drove off to Gatwick to spend the night in a hotel before flying the next morning to Gran Canaria to honeymoon for a week.

Things were looking up in Pam and Graham's life. Two years had passed since their wedding day. Rose and Ben had moved to Purbrook, just a short drive along the A3 to Portsmouth. Pam had managed to get her transfer to Portsmouth police station. They had saved enough for a deposit on a detached three-bedroom house. Graham was still getting his dreams, although the ferocity of anguish that went with them had reduced them to a bearable level. A month had passed since he had advertised his services to analyse persistent disturbing dreams that people might be experiencing, but so far, no interest in his advert had been shown. He had made up his mind that he would give it one last try and advertise in three of the most popular daily papers, and if there was no response, he would admit defeat and pursue it no longer.

Mrs Peters was getting a little suspicious about Pam's visits to the bathroom. If she wasn't mistaken, there would soon be an addition to the family. One morning, when Pam was getting ready for work, Mrs Peters enquired about her health. 'Are you sure you should go to work today, Pam? You look awful.'

'I feel awful, Mother. I can't stop being sick.'

'I don't think you have anything to worry about, but when you finish work tonight, I want you to pop into a chemist and get yourself a pregnancy test.'

'Oh my god, do you think I am going to have a baby?'

'I wouldn't be surprised, dear, but don't tell Graham until you're absolutely sure.'

'I don't think I can wait until tonight. Maybe I will call into a chemist shop while I am on duty. I will phone you later if the news is positive.' That morning, she was policing the local shopping mall. True to her word, she popped into the chemist and came out with the pregnancy test. She made her way to the public toilets, she locked herself in a cubicle then opened the package and read the instructions. She obeyed the instructions and sat on the toilet seat and waited. It wasn't long before her result began to show. 'Blue,' she said to herself, 'it's blue, I'm preggers.' Before she left that cubicle, she had informed her mother and father and Graham's mother and even his grandmother, but she didn't call Graham; she wanted that moment to be special.

That evening, Graham returned home from the laboratory, and as soon as he stepped through the door, he sensed there was something in the air. The ladies were fussing over him for no apparent reason.

'Okay, Mother, what's up?'

'Nothing, dear,' she replied in that innocent voice that made him even more certain that something was.

'Pam, what is it? Let me guess—we have a moving date from the estate agent?'

'Not to my knowledge, dear.'

'You two are up to something, I can feel it.'

Pam's secret was bursting to come out. It was no good; she couldn't conceal it any longer. 'How many people in this room, Graham?' she teased.

'Three,' he replied. 'Me, you, and Mother.'

'Are you sure?' she said, continuing the teasing.

'Unless someone is hiding behind the curtain, then yes, I am.'

Mrs Peters was loving the way that her daughter-in-law was teasing her son. 'He is not a very good counter, is he, Pam?' she said, helping out with the act.

'Let me count for you, dear,' said Pam. 'I can see you have had a hard day. Let's see—there is you, me, and Mother, but wait, who is this hiding in my tummy?'

'You're kidding me. Tell me you are pulling my leg. You're not, are you? Yippee!' he yelled. 'I am going to be a dad, and you are going to be a mum, and, Mother, you are going to be a grandmother! I must tell Grandma, and, Pam, you have to ring your parents—they will be over the moon!'

'I already have. You were the last to know.'

'I feel like celebrating. Let's all go out for a meal.' The ladies didn't need any persuading, and the three of them spent the evening eating and romancing about babies, what sex it would be, what name they would call it. They had an evening that was truly memorable.

Over the following month, life in the Peters household became rather hectic. The estate agent finally released the keys to their new house. What with measuring up for curtains, shopping for furniture, being available for carpet fitters and the gas engineer, and getting the phone connected, as well as visiting the doctor and booking in for the antenatal clinic, there didn't seem to be enough time left to think of anything else. Five weeks after Pam informed Graham that she was pregnant, they finally moved into their new home. That weekend, Pam's parents paid a visit. Pam showed her mother around the house, while Graham and her father took a stroll in the garden.

'I have noticed you haven't got a telly yet, Graham,' said Ben, whose first instinct when walking into a front room was to switch on the box and plonk himself in front of it until he heard the words 'Dinner is served.'

'I don't have time to watch telly at the moment, sir.'

'Please, Graham, call me Ben. You don't have to stand on ceremony with me.'

'Okay, from now on, it is Ben.'

'Good. Mother and I were wondering what to get you as a moving-in present. So now we know—a television. What size would you like?'

'I think you had better ask Pam. She will be watching it more than me.'

'You're learning quickly the secrets of a peaceful life, my boy.'

They both laughed then returned to the house. Another week went by, and it seemed like they had lived there all their lives. Graham was busy converting the spare room into an office, while Pam was turning the little bedroom into the baby's room. He had completely forgotten that he had let his advert in the daily papers run another month, so when his mother phoned and said a woman had phoned and wanted to speak to him, his first words were, 'What about?'

'The advert you put in the papers, of course. I asked her for her phone number and said you would call her back. I also took her name, a Miss Clarke.'

'Thank you, Mother. I will phone her later.' All the feelings of his own experience flooded back into his memory. *Do I want this extra pressure in my life now that my life is so much better than it was?* he asked himself. *Or should I listen to this woman's story?* It was no contest. His enquiring nature won the day, and he phoned her that evening. 'Miss Clarke, my name is Graham Peters. Thank you for contacting me. In what way can I help you?'

'I feel a little embarrassed, really, but after I had read your advert, I thought you might help me understand my dreams.'

'Don't feel embarrassed, Miss Clarke. The reason I am making enquiries is that I have been through exactly the same experiences myself, with a most extraordinary outcome, and I want to know if there are other people out there in the big wide world who have experienced similar dreams. If, however, you feel uncomfortable with the way my investigation is proceeding, then please tell me, and we will cease immediately.'

'Thank you, Mr Peters. That goes a long way to relieving my fears.'

'Good,' Graham said decisively. 'Now you tell me exactly what your dreams are telling you, and I will decide if I think it is worth pursuing. Take your time and try to remember as much as you can.'

'I don't quite know where to start,' she said, sounding as though she needed a little nudge.

'Okay,' said Graham, 'how often do you have these dreams? Once a month, weekly, every night?'

'Most nights,' she replied.

'And are they always the same?'

'They vary slightly, but the same theme is always present.'

'What is that underlying theme?'

'There is a man—I can't identify who he is. He is rowing a small boat on a lake. He has a young person in the boat with him. They are heading to an island in the middle of the lake. What do you think it means?'

'I have no idea, but together we will try and find out. Tell me, do you sense any feelings while you are dreaming?'

'Yes, I do.'

'What kind of feelings, Miss Clarke?'

'Feelings of self-loathing, disgust, even fear. It's getting to the stage where I dread going to bed at night.'

Graham sensed that telltale cracking in her voice that told him she was close to tears. 'Take a second to gather your composure before we continue,'

'I am all right now,' she said. 'It was just a small case of self-pity,' she bravely admitted.

'Please continue.'

'Are your parents still alive, Miss Clarke?'

'My mother is. She has Alzheimer's and is in a nursing home. My father died when I was eight years old.'

'How did he die?'

'He had gone fishing in the local lake. They said he must have fallen in and couldn't climb back up the steep bank. It was midwinter and freezing cold that day. They said the cold water was too much for him to bear.'

'Where did they live before he died, Miss Clarke?'

'Swanbridge—it's a small town near Crowley.'

'I shouldn't ask a lady this, but can you tell me how old you are?'

'That is quite all right. I have no problem telling you that I am forty-two.'

'And how old was your father when he died?'

'Oddly enough, he was forty-two as well, but why do you want to know all this?'

'At this particular moment in time, no reason whatsoever, what I am trying to do is to build up a picture of your past to see if there is anything that might have triggered these horrible dreams. It is a similar process to looking for a needle in the proverbial haystack. One last question, was your childhood a happy one?'

'Very happy, thank you. I had many friends. They were always around our house. When they weren't, Daddy was taking us out in his camper van or going on rambles. It was great. I really miss those days.'

'I think we will leave it at that for today. I will investigate your dreams. I make no promises as to solving what is causing your torment, and I must warn you that sometimes my investigations may turn up something you don't necessarily want to hear, so if you don't wish me to continue, please tell me now, one last question—who would you say you looked like, your mother or your father or neither?'

'That is easy, I have been told many times that I was my father's double. I see no reason why you shouldn't continue. After all, it's only a dream. What on earth could you find that would upset me?' she laughingly replied.

'Very well, Miss Clarke. I will go ahead with my investigation and will let you know as soon as I have some answers for you.'

She thanked Graham, but in truth, she thought all those irrelevant questions didn't add up to a tin of beans.

Graham, however, ended the conversation feeling very uneasy about what he had just heard. The one piece of information Miss Clarke was not aware of was the thought DNA that she had inherited from her father. He hoped he was wrong, but his instinct told him differently. He roamed around the house in deep thought.

Pam brought him back to the real world. 'And I said, "Would you like a cup of coffee?" What on earth were you thinking about?'

'Make the coffee, and I will sit down and tell you about it. I could certainly do with a second opinion.'

Pam made the coffee then sat down and listened to her husband, relating the phone conversation with Miss Clarke. She listened with the same intensity that she did when Graham was recalling his own story on the very first time they had set eyes on each other.

'What do you think, Pam?'

'I think . . .' She hesitated for a moment. 'I think you should get in touch with Martin Penn and see if he can uncover something from her family's past. If anyone can, he can.'

'That, Mrs Peters, is a very good idea. I will phone him tomorrow during my lunch break.'

CHAPTER FIFTEEN

Martin was busy trying to catch up with his backlog of reports when the phone rang. 'DI Penn speaking.'

'Is that Martin speaking?'

'Yes, who is asking?'

'It is me, Martin—Graham Peters.'

'Graham, how are you?' He seemed genuinely happy to hear from him. 'How is Pam, and how's married life treating you?'

'She is on cloud nine because we will be expecting our first baby later in the year.'

'That is terrific. I was only thinking about you the other day when I read your advert in the paper. Have you had any takers yet?'

'That is what I am phoning about, Martin, Pam, and I wondered if you could help us?'

'Of course I will, if I can.'

'I don't want to send you off on some wild goose chase, so for now, I will ask you to do just one thing for me.'

'Go ahead, Graham, I must say this sounds intriguing.'

'Could you contact the Crowley police, and ask them if they have any outstanding cases of children going missing from the years 1962 to 1972. I don't want to elaborate any further until you have found out. I might be completely wrong—please God that I am—but if I am not, I could be handing you the biggest case of your career.'

'Christ, Graham, what on earth have you uncovered?' Graham certainly had a knack for stirring Martin's interest.

'I will give you everything that I know on the outcome of what you come back to me with.'

'Leave it with me. I will get back to you as soon as I have something. Give me your phone number. It might take a day or two, so be patient.'

'Thanks, Martin, I know you will do your best,' said Graham gratefully.

'I will speak to you later. Say hello to Pam for me and tell her I am delighted for you both regarding the baby.'

As soon as Graham had hung up, Martin contacted Crowley police station. He introduced himself and asked to speak to a senior detective.

'DCI Paul Granger speaking. Who are you again?' came a less-than-friendly voice.

'My name is DI Martin Penn. I am stationed at Hamwell. What I am ringing for might be nothing, or it might be the biggest case you have ever handled.'

'Okay, you have got my attention now. Let's have it, mate?'

Sorry to trouble you, mate, thought Martin, then asked him the question: 'Could you tell me if you have any outstanding cases of missing children from the years 1962 to 1972?'

'I will pop down to records and ask them. I will get back to you tomorrow. If there is something happening on my patch, mate, I want to know about it,' Paul said in a threatening way.

'If I have any relevant information I will indeed share it with you, *mate*, but I don't care what rank you are. If you want to get on with me, you had better sharpen up your communication skills.' And with that, Martin hung up on him.

The following morning, Paul was in possession of the information that Martin had requested. He phoned Martin. His voice sounded as though he had to eat a large helping of humble pie.

'Martin, it's Paul Granger. I have the info you requested,'

'Hi, Paul. Thanks for getting back to me so promptly. What have you turned up?'

'It looks as though you might be on to something. Four children went missing within that time frame—three girls, their ages range between eight to eleven, and one seven-year-old boy. None of them have ever been found.'

'Wow! Thanks for that, Paul. I have to ring someone now, but hang loose—I think your common-sense approach to investigating a crime may soon be tested, so try and find out as much about the children who are missing as possible, and I will get back to you ASAP.'

That evening, Martin phoned Graham. He related the news from Crowley to him and asked how it changed the situation.

'Considerably,' he said in a grave voice. 'I need to meet you, Martin. What I have to say I would rather not say on the phone.'

'Of course not, but Crowley is outside my jurisdiction, so I will have to bring a detective with me from the Crowley station.'

'That is no problem. I do hope he has an open mind.'

'He is certainly going to need it while dealing with you,' laughed Martin.

'I am having a day off on Monday, and I am taking Pam to the antenatal class, but I have the afternoon free if that is convenient.'

'It should be, I will let you know if I can't make it, give me your address and I will see you Monday.'

Martin walked down to the chief's office. He felt he needed to inform him of events so far.

'Well, of course you have got to go,' he said. 'Those Crowley boys wouldn't stand a chance against Graham without you to help them.'

'Thanks, Chief, I agree. I don't know what they will make of Graham.' He left the chief's office and phoned Paul. He arranged to pick him up at Crowley police station at 1 p.m. on Monday and drive him to Graham's house. He set off early from Hamwell, allowing for heavy traffic that never materialised, which meant he arrived at Crowley at just after midday. He checked in at the desk and asked the desk sergeant to put a call out for Paul. A tall man in his late forties came down and greeted him.

'You must be Martin. I wasn't expecting you for another hour. I was just going to snatch a bite to eat. If you haven't eaten yet, why don't you join me?'

'You don't have to ask me twice. Lead the way, when in Rome,' Martin replied.

During lunch, they swapped information and general police banter about this and that, then Paul asked the million-dollar question. 'This chap that we are going to see, who is he?'

'He is the most remarkable man that I have ever met. The first time that I met him, he was in a cemetery. He had just dug up a one-hundred-year-old grave and retrieved a substantial amount of stolen gold. What was I doing there? Well, I will tell you. I was arresting him when we finally interviewed him, and I asked him how he knew the loot was in the grave. He said that he had dreamt it. He then went on to explain that the thought DNA that he had inherited from his great-great-grandfather Arthur Tidwell had materialised in his dreams, and it was Arthur that had robbed and murdered a jeweller in the year 1911. It was a fascinating case. I checked his evidence thoroughly, and the only conclusion I could come to was that he was telling the truth. His dreams had been causing him great stress. He had this idea that if he returned the gold to the relatives of the jeweller, his horrible dreams would go.'

Paul listened intently. 'And did they?' he asked.

'Oh yes, we arranged for him to hand over the loot in the briefing room. He insisted that he apologise personally for the grief that his family had inflicted on the jeweller's family. If there was any doubt about his honesty before, there sure wasn't afterwards. While he was apologising, his face went white and he started to sweat, then the voice of his great-great-grandfather took over. I don't mind telling you it scared the shit out of me.'

'That is some story, Martin,' said Paul. 'Now tell me the truth—you made it up, didn't you?'

'No, he is now advertising in the papers for people who have experienced the same kind of dreams to contact him with the aim to help them.'

'I read that advert,' Paul said. 'That's him, is it?'

'That is right. Apparently someone has contacted him, and their dreams are making him feel very uneasy, so that is why he has called us in, the Ghostbusters.'

'I am looking forward to this,' said Paul with an air of anticipation.

'If you have finished your lunch, let's go,'

An hour later, they were knocking on Graham's door. Pam answered it. 'Martin, how are you? It is so good to see you.'

'I am good, Pam, but you must lay off of the pies,' he said, looking down at her tummy that was showing definite signs of pregnancy. 'This is Paul Granger from Crowley station. Pam sat in with me when we interviewed Graham and ended up marrying him,'

'I am pleased to meet you, Pam,' Paul said formally, feeling like the odd man out.

'Come on in. Graham is in his office. Let me take you to him, then I will make you all a coffee.'

Martin introduced Paul to Graham, who eyed him up and down. His first impression was that he reminded him of the baboon.

'Sit yourselves down, gentlemen. Before I start, let me first say that at this moment in time, what I am about to say is purely a hunch, although finding out that four children went missing between the dates that I gave you very much supports my hunch.'

Pam walked in with coffee and biscuits. She placed the tray on the table and left the men to it.

Graham continued, 'A woman contacted me, saying she was experiencing continuous reoccurring dreams. In her dreams, she felt fear and self-loathing. Her dreams featured a man in a boat rowing across a lake. In the boat, with him was a child. I think at this stage I should inform you, Paul, that what I am researching is whether it is possible for the thoughts of a dead person to manifest later in a relative many years in the future. As for myself, I am 100 per cent sure it can, as my own experience has proved. I have checked my dates. My client—I will call her my client, although strictly speaking she isn't, as I am not charging her for my services—was born in 1972. The children went missing at various dates within the ten years before. The father died when she was eight years old. He drowned in a lake. I asked myself if it was an accident or if he could not live with his guilt any longer. Before he died, my client said he liked to take her and her friends out in his camper van. It might have been totally innocent, or did he have an unhealthy interest in being around young children, and was it him she was seeing in a boat with children? Innocent or guilty, I think it needs investigating because there are some parents out there who need some sort of closure to their grief. Tell me, what you think? Do you think it is worth investigating?'

'Do you have any idea where the lake is?' asked Paul.

'No, I don't. All I can tell you is that there is an island in the middle of it, and it is probably in the vicinity of Crowley. She said they lived in Swanbridge,'

'That could be helpful,' said Paul, writing it down in his notebook. 'I don't suppose you have their family name?'

'Yes, I do. It's Clarke.'

Again he wrote the name in his notebook. 'I will check to see if anything is known when I get back to the station.'

'Keep me informed?' said Martin, sensing Paul was about to take over the case.

'If I get any more information, I will give it to Martin and let him pass it to you, Paul,' said Graham, much to Martin's relief. 'One other thing that might help you—I believe he liked to go fishing, so you might want to check out the fishing lakes in that area first.'

'Can you give me the name of your client, Graham?'

'No, that information stays with me. She trusts me, and if there is any more information to come from her, I think I am the best person to get it.'

'I agree,' said Martin.

'As you wish' said Paul, not entirely happy about it.

They stayed with Pam and Graham for another hour. Pam was asking Martin lots of questions about her ex-colleagues at Hamwell, while Paul was getting more and more fidgety and couldn't wait to leave.

They eventually got away about half an hour before the rush hour started. Martin asked Paul how he was going to proceed with his enquiries.

'Your man Graham hasn't really given us much. He says he is only working on a hunch, and it could be pure coincidence that four children went missing around that time, so what are we left with, some woman's dreams? I will make some enquiries regarding her father and check out how many fishing lakes are in the area with an island in the middle. Other than that, I don't know what else I can do.'

'You will keep me informed about anything you find out, won't you?' said Martin, feeling a little uneasy about the amount of effort his newfound friend was going to give to the enquiry.

'Of course I will.'

I bet you will, thought Martin.

He dropped Paul off at Crowley police station and made his way to Hamwell.

On arriving back at Hamwell, he parked up and sat in his car and lit up a cigarette. He thought about what had transpired that day. Was Graham on to something, or was this a desperate attempt to add more proof to his theory of what had happened to him? And what about Paul? He didn't radiate much confidence in his ability to investigate something that wasn't even a case yet, just a hunch based solely on a dream. Martin felt a little put out by not being in charge of the investigation.

CHAPTER SIXTEEN

Two weeks had gone by, and Martin hadn't heard from either Paul or Graham. He wondered whether Graham had heard from Paul, so he phoned him and asked.

'No, I haven't,' he said, 'have you?'

'Not me either. He is dragging his heels a bit, isn't he?' Martin complained.

'I can't continue until he gets back to us with his findings,' said Graham.

'I will call him now and get back to you.'

Paul picked up his phone. 'DCI Granger speaking.'

'Paul, it's Martin. Have you made any progress with the missing children?'

'I have checked out Mr Clarke. He is squeaky clean, and as far as lakes in our area are concerned, there are twenty-two, and seventeen of them have an island in them, so I am sorry—we just don't have the manpower to investigate them based just on a hunch.'

'I thought you were supposed to keep me informed,' said Martin, who was more than a little annoyed.

'I would have if I had something to give you, but I haven't.'

Martin ended the conversation without speaking another word.

He immediately rang Graham back and told him of Paul's feeble attempt at an investigation.

'No problem, Martin. We will leave the baboons to play in the monkey house. I think I will try and meet up with Miss Clarke. Perhaps if I disclose my own experience with her, she just might open up and air some of her dirty washing, so to speak.'

'I will be there for you if you need me. Good luck,' said Martin, offering his support.

The next day, Graham rang Miss Clarke and arranged a meeting at her house. It was Saturday. They hadn't anything planned, so he asked Pam if she would like to accompany him; he thought it might put Miss Clarke more at ease if a woman was with him. They arrived at her house mid- morning; she opened the door gingerly and then invited them in. She was a woman with a very nervous disposition, and Graham knew right away that he must tread very carefully if he was to extract any information from her that could be of any use to him. How was he going to start? He decided to tell her of his own dreams and the revelation of finding out that his distant relative was a murderer and thief and how he had uncovered the truth—by being caught in a grave holding the loot—how he felt that the thought DNA that he had inherited was trying to tell him to right the wrong of his distant relative and return the loot to the family of the rightful owner, and when he eventually completed his tale of how the dreams and the guilt that accompanied them subsided, he suggested that could it be possible that in some strange way, her dreams were also trying to tell her something.

She listened intently, and he felt he had touched a nerve.

'To get to your problem, I have to ask you some very searching questions.'

'Very well,' she said, sounding rather nervous.

'I will start by asking you, what is your first name?'

'Clare.'

'I am Graham, and this is my wife, Pam. We haven't named the little fellow who is hiding in her tummy yet.'

Clare gave a nervous laugh.

'Tell me, why hasn't an attractive lady like you got herself married yet?'

'I can't seem to find a man whom I can trust,'

'Why do you think that is, Clare?' Graham sensed there was something trapped deep within her psyche that she was either in denial of or she was too ashamed to admit to herself. It was something to do with her father, he was certain of that, and so this is the line of investigation he pursued.

'When I last spoke to you, Clare, you put a lot of emphasis on how happy your childhood was and what a fun person your father had been. Was that the complete truth, or were you only saying that to veil a hidden torment?' He had touched a nerve because she stared at him like a rabbit in the headlights; he had just gained access into her very soul. Complete silence followed for a long thirty seconds, then she cracked.

'Why did he do that? I was only a child. He said it was because he loved me, but it hurt so much, and when I tried to tell Mother, she slapped me and told me not to be so wicked.'

Pam rushed to her aid, putting her arm around her and trying to console her by telling her she had nothing to feel guilty about. She had only been a child at the time, and sad as it was, there were children at this present moment in time that were going through the same experience, and it was twice as hard to bear when it was a relative carrying out the abuse.

It gave Graham no pleasure in knowing he had made a crucial breakthrough, but his suspicions of what kind of person Clare's father was and what he might be guilty of seemed increasingly more likely.

'Would you mind if I made us a coffee, Clare?' said Graham. He nodded at Pam to stay with her for support.

'Your husband is very kind, isn't he?' she sniffed.

'He is the most wonderful man I know, Clare. Not all men are bad, and you too might be able to find yourself a loving man. Now you are beginning to release your childhood baggage.'

'Do you really think so, Pam?' Clare said, her red eyes looking up at Pam for the first time since she had broken down.

'I am convinced of it,' said Pam.

'I feel that I have had a heavy load lifted off my brain, Pam. It feels like I am—how can I put it—liberated.'

'That is good, Clare. What you must do now is not let your father ruin your life any more and get out there and enjoy life, and if you have any doubts about a relationship, then just walk away, and phone me if you need any advice.'

Graham walked in with the coffee and handed Clare and Pam a cup each. 'I didn't know whether you took sugar, Clare, so I put some in an egg cup for you,'

'Thank you,' she said. She looked so pathetic and vulnerable as she sat sipping her coffee. Pam pulled Graham to one side. 'We can't leave her like this, Graham. I would never forgive myself if something should happen to her.'

'What are suggesting, dear?' asked Graham.

'Taking her back home with us until she is strong enough to cope by herself.'

'But we don't have a spare bed. Or are you expecting us all to sleep in the same bed?'

That remark earned him a highly deserved dig in the ribs by Pam's elbow.

'We could go to your mother's and ask her if we could borrow your old bed. I am sure she wouldn't mind—we could put it in the baby's room for her.'

'Before you say anything to Clare, let me go and okay it with Mother.'

Graham walked into the garden and phoned his mother. He explained the situation, and she was only too happy to help. He arranged to pick the bed up later that day. He ended the call by telling his mother that he loved her then went back to Pam and Clare. He never spoke; he just nodded to say that everything had been arranged.

Clare gave no resistance to Pam's suggestion, and that evening, all three of them were sitting in the front room of Graham's house. Two days later, Pam's infectious personality began to rub off on Clare. They went shopping together. Clare particularly liked looking in the baby shops and picking up the little booties and baby clothes. Laughing with another human being was such a new experience for her and so therapeutic. She liked it and wanted more. She knew it couldn't last, and that evening, she thanked them for their hospitality, but it was time for her to return home.

Graham was caught by surprise by what Clare had said. He was about to put the next stage of his investigation into action, and that involved Clare's participation. Pam disappeared into the kitchen, and Graham followed.

'You must persuade her to stay for a couple more days, Pam.'

'Why?' said Pam, somewhat confused.

'I need to find the lake that keeps cropping up in her dreams, and if it is her father's shame and guilt she is experiencing, it just might trigger a memory in her subconscious. I know it's a long shot, but she is the only hope we have of locating it.'

'How on earth is she going to do that?' Pam asked.

'Do you remember my experience? The day I walked down Broad Street and how I said that I had the feeling that I had been there before even though I had never even been to Hamwell before, let alone Broad Street? Well, I hadn't, but Arthur Tidwell certainly had, and it was his memories I was experiencing. If we can persuade her to visit the lakes one by one, it might trigger a memory or a feeling that she has inherited. Who knows what might happen? But it is worth a try.'

'That dear husband is one heck of a long shot, even for you.'

She isn't aware of the four missing children, and I don't think it would be a good idea to tell her, at least not yet, but it is the only chance we will get to prove our theory of what happened to those poor children, and Crowley police station wouldn't be able to find them even if we dumped them on their doorstep, so, Pam, what do you think?'

'I agree. It is the least we can do in an attempt to alleviate the suffering of the children's families. Also, we mustn't forget the reason we are doing this in the first place—that is to free Clare from the demons that visit her in her sleep. I will talk to her tomorrow while you are at work and, hopefully, get her to stay over the weekend.'

The following day, Pam went into action, trying to persuade Clare to stay over for the weekend. She started by saying what good company Clare was, and asking her to please stay for the weekend. Then she asked if her bad dreams had gone.

'I wish they had,' said Clare. 'But last night I had a nasty one.'

'Graham would like to try an experiment with you. He seems to think that the key to unlocking what is trapped in your thought DNA has something to do with the lake. What he would like to do is to visit the lakes around where you used to live to see if it triggers any memories. It will be fun,' said Pam. 'We can stop for lunch. Oh, do say you will come, Clare. It will be fun.'

'Putting it like that, Pam, how can I refuse?'

'Oh goody,' said Pam, laying it on thick. 'Now let's go shopping.'

That night, in bed, Pam told Graham how she managed to get Clare to stay for the weekend without averting any suspicion to the real reason.

'You, Mrs Peters, are devious, but what a team we have become.'

'And you, Mr Peters, are a lot of things, but one thing you are not is boring,'

A kiss goodnight signalled the end of the day.

CHAPTER SEVENTEEN

Saturday morning, Graham sat at the end of his bed. He had just awoken from a dream. It was the dream that involved the last piece of the jigsaw that he hoped would lay his demons to rest—the gold chain and the heart-shaped locket with the word *love* etched into it. In truth, he had given up on solving the mystery of where it might be. Pam and Clare were already up. He could smell bacon frying. He had a quick wash and shave then put on his weekend clothes. 'No collar and tie today,' he said to himself, then slipped on a pair of jeans and a T-shirt then went downstairs to the ladies. 'That bacon smells good, Pam. Two eggs for me, Clare,' he ordered.

'Of course, master,' Clare joked. 'Would you also like me to eat it for you?'

'And that's enough cheek from you, my girl,' he came back with.

'Did you hear that, Pam? I am his girl now. You will have to watch him carefully.'

'He is asking for a whack over the head with a frying pan,' said Pam, continuing the humour.

The three of them sat down to breakfast, and Graham started to explain what they were going to do and why. He started by saying that he felt the answer to resolving her bad dreams had a connection with water. Diverting from the real reason for visiting the lakes, he made out that when her father died, it had been in water, and perhaps the two coincidences were related. He had done his homework in the week and knew roughly where the lakes were to be located. They set off for Swanbridge at just after 10 a.m., and by 2 p.m., they had visited six lakes. None of them had the desired effect on Clare that Graham had hoped for. They stopped for lunch in a country pub; the big breakfast had ruined their appetite for a full-blown dinner so they all settled for a ploughman's lunch. Graham sat waiting in the car while the ladies powdered their noses. They resumed their quest at 2.45 p.m.; they had visited two more lakes without any joy. Graham was beginning to think it was all a wild goose chase. They persevered. It was late afternoon before they reached Cray Farm carp lake, That was the sign at the beginning of the lane that led to the lake: 'Cray Farm carp lake, £5 per day, apply at farm house for ticket'. There was a locked barrier across the lane to prevent vehicles from going down without permission. Graham decided to leave the car at the end of the lane and walk down to the lake. The lake was about a hundred yards down the lane, and it seemed to get narrower the further they went down it.

'The farmer was certainly not going to retire on the proceeds of the fishermen who fished this lake,' said Pam. Looking at the length of the grass, it looked like nobody had been there for ages. They walked to the water's edge. Graham noticed the small island in the centre. It was plain to see that nobody had set foot on it for a very long time, as it was covered with bramble. There was about fifteen yards of water separating the island from the bank. 'It's a desolate place,' remarked Pam.

'Can we go now please?' said Clare.

'What is it, Clare?' asked Graham. The way she said it made his heart beat faster.

'I don't know. I am getting a feeling that this is not a nice place. I feel I have been here before, but I am certain I never have. I can see a small jetty with a boat tethered to it—it was over there.' She pointed to a corner to the left side of where they were standing.

'Do you think that this is where your father drowned?'

'I am not certain of it. It could be, but it is making me feel very uncomfortable,' said Clare giving a visible shudder.

Graham felt his gamble had paid off. 'Come on, let's go home. I think I have put you through enough for one day. Let's pray that this pilgrimage will finally help you to banish your bad dreams.'

They walked back to the car then drove home. Clare hardly spoke a word; she was trying to fathom out why she had those awful feelings while standing on the bank of the lake. When they arrived home, Graham attempted to explain to Clare that what she had experienced was not her memories but the memories of her father. It was his thoughts that she had inherited in the DNA that was speaking to her. And in his opinion, because her father had died in a violent way, that was the reason the feelings were so vivid. She accepted his explanation without question; to her it made sense. Graham cast his mind back to his first encounter with Jeff and Mary Goldstein and how he had to disguise the real reason for his enquiries in an attempt to reach the truth. He couldn't tell Clare, but he was certain that her father had murdered four local children and hid their bodies either in that lake, or more likely, thinking of her dreams where she kept seeing a man in a boat with a child, he had buried them on that island. It certainly was not the explanation he had just given Clare. How could it be? Her father's DNA had been in her body long before he had died.

The next day, they drove Clare home. She thanked them both for their hospitality, saying she would miss them. Pam said they were not far away and if they had a little girl, they would call her Clare and would come up to see her and bring the baby with them.

'That will be lovely,' said Clare. 'I will look forward to that.'

'Just remember what I told you,' said Pam. 'Get out and enjoy life, and remember, not all men are bad, and you have a lot to offer. You are beautiful and intelligent, the perfect recipe for sweeping a man off of his feet.'

That made Clare laugh. They then hugged, and their eyes showed signs of emotion. With that, Pam and Graham departed for home.

On the way back home, they were silent for a long time, then Pam spoke.

'I do hope we are wrong, but I fear that the evidence is stacking up to the contrary,'

Graham agreed, saying, 'Sometimes I wish that I had never put that stupid advert in the paper.'

'Don't go talking like that. Of course you were right. It was right for you and for Clare, but mainly, if the children are found, for their long-suffering parents, so let's not have any more of this negativity.'

'You're absolutely right, Pam. Sometimes I need you to give me a kick up the pants just to keep me going.' He needed her to be strong for him on occasions, and this was one of them.

CHAPTER EIGHTEEN

The phone rang on Martin Penn's desk; he recognised the voice immediately.

'Is that DI Penn?' the voice on the other end said.

'No, Graham, it is not. It is DCI Penn.'

'Congratulations, Martin, you deserve it,'

'Hey, I'm sorry we didn't get a result on that theory of yours. What can I do for you this time?' said Martin.

'I won't beat about the bush, Martin. I have located the lake where I think the children were buried.'

'How on earth have you managed to do that, Graham?' said Martin. Although it seemed unbelievable, this was Graham he was talking to.

'Working on my own experience, I played a hunch. Pam and I befriended the woman in question. I found out that she was abused by her father. She was in such a state after she revealed her secret to us that we invited her to stay with us, fearing she might do something silly if we left her on her own. She bonded with Pam immediately, and by the end of the week, she was completely relaxed. She was still having her dreams, and so I suggested we try an experiment. I said to her if we tried to locate the lake where her father died, it might help to bring a closure to her torment. Of course, my motive for locating the lake was far more sinister. Last Saturday morning, we visited numerous lakes. Every one of the lakes failed to give her the response that I was hoping for. However, in the afternoon, we eventually came to a lake where my old friend déjà vu took over. As she was standing beside the edge of the lake, she started to complain that she was feeling ill at ease. Saying she wanted to leave, she pointed to one end of the lake, and even though she said she had never been there before, she said there was once a little jetty there and could imagine a boat tethered to it. Of course she was totally unaware that four children were missing.'

'You have been a busy boy, haven't you, Graham? It seems you may have cracked it. I am going to the chief super now and inform him of what you have just told me, so leave it with me, and I will get back to you as soon as I have some news.'

Martin immediately headed for the chiefs office. His door was wide open, and he gave it a gentle knock then walked in.

The chief put down his pen and looked up at his DCI.

'Yes, what is it, Martin?'

'It is Graham Peters, sir. He has located the lake.'

'Is it possible that he has identified the right lake?' the chief super asked.

'If it was anybody else telling me the story, I would tell them to shove off,' said Martin, 'but we are talking about Graham Peters, and I learnt a long time ago not to take what he tells me with a pinch of salt.'

'Okay, Martin, I will contact my opposite number at Crowley and see what help he can give us.'

That afternoon, the chief super phoned Crowley police station. Chief Superintendent John Groves answered it, and he listened carefully to what was being said. 'Didn't we investigate this a while ago?' he said.

'You sort of investigated it. Your DCI Granger browsed over it and decided they didn't have the manpower to investigate every lake in Crowley, which was fair comment, but now we have narrowed it down to one lake. Surely we can send a team in, can't we?' said Ronald.

'I don't know what it's like in Hamwell, Ronald, but down here we have to be very careful how we spend our money,' said John.

'Don't be under any illusion that we don't have the same problems here, but something as big as this has got to be worth opening up the purse strings for. Don't you agree, John? And if we are right, what a scoop for you and your station.'

'All right, Ronald, you have convinced me. You can be very persuasive with someone else's money, can't you?'

'Don't be such a scrooge. Just think of the headlines in the papers—"Chief Superintendent John Groves and His Team of Detectives Solve the Mystery of Four Children Who Have Been Missing for Nearly Forty Years".'

'All right, all right, I get it,' said John, imagining the glory that would be heading his way if the children could actually be found on his watch.

'My DCI, Martin Penn, must be there with his contact, Graham Peters, whom you will find invaluable at the crime scene, if indeed there is one,' said Ronald. 'I might put in an appearance myself, if it's okay with you, John.'

'Of course, Ronald. Now let's set a date. Is this Friday all right for you and your team?'

'I will confirm that with you tomorrow.'

'You haven't told me where this lake is yet, Ronald.'

'That is because I don't know. My DCI will furnish me with all the info we need. You just organise a couple of divers and possibly some heavies with shovels.'

'Will do,' said John, still pumped up at the thought of a major crime being solved by his station.

The chief called Martin into his office. He spoke very decisively. 'I want you and Graham available next Friday. I want the location of the lake. I will be joining you. We will have divers and a digging crew. Let us pray we find something, or we will be the laughingstock of the whole force.'

Graham knocked on Professor Irvin's office door. A loud voice blasted out, 'Enter. Yes, Graham, what can I do for you?'

'You know my other project that I am working on? Well, I am sure I have located where the children are buried. I have informed the police and they want me to be there at the search.'

'Well of course you must be there. When do they want you?'

'Friday.'

'It's a bit short notice, but of course you must go. I do hope you find them.'

'Something inside me wants to find them, but another part of me would like them to turn up alive, Professor.'

'What I was thinking, Graham, is if they find the children, your theory on DNA thought transference would have been proven beyond any shadow of a doubt, and that, Graham, in my opinion, is a great scientific discovery.'

CHAPTER NINETEEN

Friday morning, the farmer who owned Cray Farm fishing lake was asked to leave the barrier up for access. Police vehicles of all shapes and sizes gathered around the bank. Martin introduced John to Graham.

'This exercise is costing a small fortune, young man. I hope it's going to be worth it.'

'So do I sir, for the sake of the parents of those children who have been tormented and for decades of not knowing what happened to them.'

'A noble thought—alas, we can't allow ourselves the luxury of sentiment in the police force,' said John.

Graham pointed to where Clare said she thought the jetty was and suggested the divers start from there. Two men in diving suits waddled down to the water's edge—they resembled two giant penguins—and they then turned around and entered the water backwards. Graham watched as they gradually submerged until all that was left were a few bubbles. Everyone stood chatting, waiting for the divers to reappear. Martin inched himself alongside Graham. 'This is it, Graham—the moment of truth. Oh well, que sera sera!'

Graham was just about to say something when a head popped up from the lake.

'Have you found anything?' John called out.

The diver lifted his goggles. 'There is a rowing boat down here,' he said. 'Pass me a rope, and I will attach it to the boat, then you can pull it up with the Land Rover.'

Martin duly obliged, and the diver disappeared for what seemed like an age. Both heads bobbed up from the water.

'We are ready when you are,' called out one of the divers, 'but for Christ's sake, take it slowly. Remember, it has probably been sitting here for a long time. Me and Jock will go down to help it on its way. I will tug the rope when we are in position.'

The Land Rover started to rev up. The rope went taut, and the boat began to slide up the bank. Everybody gathered around it. Martin spotted a letter that had appeared when the reeds had wiped off some of the mud when the boat was being dragged through them.

'Has anyone got a bucket and brush?' he shouted. Somebody opened the back of one of the vans and produced a stiff broom and a bucket. He walked down to the water's edge and filled up the bucket. 'Stand back, everybody. I don't want to get mud all over you.' He dipped the broom into the water and began to scrub. A name began to appear—SEA LARK. 'That doesn't tell us much,' said Paul Granger.

'Doesn't tell us much?' Graham said in amazement. 'What name did I give you to check out, Paul?'

'Oh, I don't know—a Mr Clarke, I think.'

'That is right,' said Graham, 'and what does that say? Sea Lark or Clark.'

Paul's face went cherry-coloured. Fortunately for him, everyone's attention was distracted by one of the officers pulling something out of the boat. 'It has still got its oar inside,' he proudly proclaimed.

Again Graham interrupted. He was pumped up now. 'That is not an oar. That is a bloody spade, and the bastard has buried them over there on the island.'

John had heard enough. 'Okay everybody, let's get over there and find those poor kids.'

If there was scepticism before they found the boat, there certainly wasn't any more. The digging team went into their task with gusto, confident of their outcome, and within four hours, the poor wretch was found, an eight-year-old girl still wearing her school uniform. Graham and Martin were sitting in Martin's car sharing a flask of coffee when Ronald and John walked over to convey the gruesome news. They opened the car door. Ronald spoke. 'We have found what we believe to be one of the missing children. Well done, Martin. Well done, Graham.'

'That goes for me too,' said John. 'You must be very happy with the outcome.'

'That is not the word that I would use to describe how I feel,' said Graham, thinking more of the plight of those poor children rather than the success of the operation.

John tried to show a modicum of humility, saying 'Of course, our thoughts should be with the parents," but really he was delighted with the outcome. He and his team at Crowley were about to become headline news. Before closing the car door, he said that they had better get back to operations, and they would keep them in touch with any further developments.

Two more hours had passed before the second child was found. She was identified by her watch and Saint Christopher, and the boys worked all through the night, and by daybreak, the island had given up all its terrible secrets. John called the operation to a close. After the last body was found, he had the foresight to arrange a mobile canteen, realising it was going to be a long, hard night and his crew would need a break every now and then. The gang of burly policemen who had worked tirelessly all night were all gathered around it, drinking hot tea. Considering their success, the mood was strangely sombre.

Later that morning, Graham phoned Pam to apologise for leaving her not knowing what was happening.

'I am almost reluctant to ask you, Graham, were our suspicions unfounded?' she asked.

'It was awful, dear—those poor children, what they must have gone through.'

'That is awful, but you must not dwell on it, dear. Think positive. Say to yourself without me, those poor kids would have been lost forever, and the suffering of their parents not knowing what happened to them would have been everlasting. Where are you now?' she enquired.

'At Crowley police station.'

'Have you had anything to eat?'

'Just a bar of chocolate.'

'Well, get yourself home, and I will have a nice hot dinner waiting for you.'

'Thank you, darling. I am ready to come home now,' he conceded.

He walked out of Crowley police station to a standing ovation from the whole team, Martin, in particular, cheered louder than anyone, and he accompanied Graham to the front door. 'Graham, you are, without doubt, the most remarkable of men, and may I say it has been a privilege to know you, and if you need me at all for anything, don't hesitate to contact me.'

'Thank you, Martin, I will.' Graham walked to his car and headed for home. He felt as though he hadn't slept for a week. Before he set off, he phoned Pam and told her he would be home within the hour. He switched on the radio and tuned it in to a music channel, then left the car park. His mind began to drift to the events of the last twenty-four hours. He thought of the closure the parents of the dead children could now have and how he took a major part in it. He felt proud of that. He then began to think about Clare. *How would he tell her the truth about her father? Should he tell her? Maybe if he didn't tell her, she might never know and live the rest of her life in complete ignorance.* His mind then drifted to his own problem— the gold locket and chain. *I wonder what happened to it?* he thought. *Did Martin and Dave Harris leave it at Annie Philpot's graveside when they emptied the contents of the sack onto the ground? It is possible. After all, it was dark. Did one of the officers take it? I don't think Martin would have, but Dave, hmm, I am not so sure. What about Arthur Tidwell/ Could he have sold it?* Graham was so deep in thought that a momentary lapse of concentration made him drift into the kerb. It woke him up instantly. He tried to correct his steering but veered across to the other side of the road. He slammed on the brake, but it was too late. The tree trunk was a far more efficient brake. His head hit the steering wheel. The horn was blasting out, but he couldn't hear it— he was out cold.

CHAPTER TWENTY

Pam paced up and down, her anger gradually turning to concern. *Where on earth has he got to? He said he would be home in an hour—that was two and a half hours ago.* She picked up the phone and rang her mother-in-law. 'Mother, is Graham with you?' Although she would be angry, she hoped the answer was yes.

'No, Pam, is everything all right?'

'He called me saying he would be home in an hour. That was nearly three hours ago. It is totally out of character for him not to let me know if he has been delayed.'

'Why don't you ring the people he was last with? They might be able to throw some light on his whereabouts.'

'That is a good idea. I will phone Martin Penn.'

She found Martin's mobile number and rang him.

'I left him at 10 a.m. I presumed he was heading home. Hey, Pam, he was brilliant, and everybody applauded him as he left the police station.'

'He will get no applause from me when I get hold of him,' she huffed.

'I will ring you later,' he said. 'If there is a problem, I might be able to help.'

'Thank you, Martin, you are a real friend,' she said, then put the phone down.

No sooner had she put it down when it rang. 'Mrs Peters?' a sombre voice said.

'Yes.' Somehow she knew what she was about to hear was not good news.

'This is Portsmouth police station. Is your husband's name Graham?'

'Yes.'

'There has been an accident. He has been admitted to Portsmouth General this morning.'

'Oh no,' she gasped. 'Please tell me he is not badly hurt.'

'That I couldn't say, ma'am. You will have to ring the hospital to find that out. The car is a compete write-off, so don't worry about picking it up. We have taken all of his personal belongings out of the car, and you can pick them up at Portsmouth police station at any time.'

'Thank you,' she said then sat down on the settee and cried her eyes out. She pulled herself together then rang her mother-in-law.

'Oh my god, is he all right, Pam?'

'I don't know, Mother. I haven't seen him yet, and the policeman said the car's a write-off.'

'I will be over there within the hour, Pam, and we will visit him together.'

'Thanks, Mother. I will be waiting for you.'

One hour later, Pam stood looking out of the front room window anxiously awaiting the arrival of her mother-in-law. She looked along the road, and it wasn't long before she spotted her car approaching, and by the time the car pulled up outside Pam's house, she was already standing on the kerbside, waiting.

'I thought we should get straight off if you don't mind, Mother,' she said, stepping into the passenger side of the car.

'Of course, Pam. Put your seatbelt on, and we will be off,' said her mother-in-law, equally anxious to learn of her son's condition.

They arrived at the hospital in the mid-afternoon and made their way to reception.

'My son was involved in a car accident this morning and was brought here,' she explained to the receptionist. 'His name is Graham Peters.'

'Please take a seat, and I will find out what ward he is in?' said the receptionist.

Ten minutes later, she called them both over to the reception desk. 'He is in Cedar Ward.' She drew them a map of the directions to the ward on a scrap of paper and pointed to the corridor they had to take. They proceeded arm in arm from one corridor to another, the sound of their high heels bounced off the grey walls. The walls were littered with paintings that looked like they had been painted by children, and the clinical smell that was present wherever they walked was intoxicating. They turned left then right and right again, passing rooms with signs outside describing what they were used for—X-rays, Oncology, Physiotherapy—the names seemed to get longer the deeper into the hospital they went. They eventually came to a cross junction in the corridors. A sign hanging from the ceiling read wards Elm and Oak to the left, Beech and Cedar to the right. They paused to read it. Their nerves reminded them of the possible reality of what might await them once they entered Cedar ward. They gripped each other's arms tight and made their way along the corridor to the ward. The doors were an off-white colour; each side had a porthole-style window. There were numerous scratches at the bottom of the doors where beds and trolleys had been pushed up against them, they peered through the windows and noticed a nurse sitting at her station, and it looked like she was filling in a report. They looked at each other, and without uttering a word, they entered the ward. The nurse looked up as they approached her, 'I am sorry,' she said apologetically. 'Visiting time is not for another three hours.' Pam explained who she was and that her husband had been admitted that morning.

'That would be the car accident,' she said in an efficient but detached manner, 'The doctor is with him now. I will take you to him.' She led them both down the ward to a bed that had a curtain around it. 'Please wait there until I speak to the doctor.' She seemed to be an age but eventually appeared with the doctor. She introduced them to him and then left to continue her duties. Doctor Visram was a man in his forties. His hair was jet black; he wore a white overall and had a stethoscope around his neck. 'Which one of you ladies is Mrs Peters?' he asked.

'We both are,' replied Graham's mother. 'I am his mother, and this is his wife. How is he, Doctor?'

'He has had a nasty bash on the head and has a small skull fracture. When he came to us, he was unconscious, and he remains in that condition now. As the bruising subsides, he should wake up, but we will keep him here for observation. If all goes well, he should be out of here in three or four days, but try not to worry—he will live. Now if you want to sit with him a while, then please go ahead.' They slid back the curtain. Graham had a bandage wrapped around his head. His eyes were closed, and a machine was monitoring his heart rate. Looking at him lying in peace gave them both a small crumb of comfort. They stayed with him for two more hours, and then the nurse came to do her rounds.

'I know how difficult this is for you,' she said, 'but why don't you both go home? There is nothing you can do. He will wake up, but it is a waiting game. You are not doing him or yourselves any favours at all by staying.'

'She is right, Pam. Come on, let's leave him to rest and visit again tomorrow.'

'You're right, Mother, but I feel so guilty leaving him like this,'

Mrs Peters put her arm around her daughter-in-law and gradually inched her away from Graham's bedside. They walked through the ward's double doors with Pam still looking back to her husband's bed in the vain hope that he would wake up and call her name. On the journey home, a thought came into Graham's mother's head: 'I ought to inform his grandmother. Otherwise, she will never forgive me if she doesn't get the opportunity to visit him. If I pick her up tomorrow morning, we can visit him in the evening.'

'How am I going to visit in the afternoon?' said Pam.

'Have you informed your parents yet, Pam?'

'No, I haven't.' said Pam. 'How could I have forgotten to do that?'

'Quite easy under the circumstances,' said Mrs Peters, refusing to condemn her daughter–in-law for her small oversight. 'Let me drive you to their house. It might be a good idea if you stayed with them for the night rather than be on your own, and I am sure they would be more than pleased to take you in the afternoon to visit him.'

'That's a good idea, Mother, are you sure you don't mind?'

'Of course not, dear. That is what families are for.' She drove Pam to her parents' house, said a quick hello, and explained the situation then returned home herself. She threw her handbag on the settee then plonked herself in an easy chair. She closed her eyes and slept soundly for two hours; she arose and made herself a coffee then phoned her mother.

'What . . . when . . . he hasn't come round yet? Oh my god, I will catch the next train down to you,'

'Hold your horses, Mother. There is no need to panic. I will drive up to you tomorrow morning and pick you up, and we will visit him together tomorrow evening.'

'Yes, yes, you do that. How is Pam taking it, the poor creature? She must be devastated.'

'It has come as a bit of a blow to her, but she is a strong girl. She will cope, I am sure, Mother.'

'I will see you tomorrow then, dear. I think I will pop out now and buy some grapes.'

'That is a good idea, Mum, and I will see you tomorrow. Bye.'

CHAPTER TWENTY-ONE

The following morning when Pam woke up, it took her a second or two to realise where she was. She sat up in bed, thinking how in the last twenty-four hours her wonderful life had been turned upside down. A knock on the door interrupted her thoughts. The door opened, and her mother's head peered around the corner. 'I have boiled you two eggs and cut the toast into fingers, just the way you like your breakfast, dear,' It was a treat for her to look after her little girl again. She would never mention it, but she missed being able to fuss over her, and as short as this stay was, she was determined to make the most of it.

'Thanks, Mum.' She smiled as she remembered her mother's fussing over her. 'I will come down right away.'

Mrs Peters set off to pick her mother up at 10 a.m., she thought she would wait for the rush-hour traffic to die down. She was a rather nervous driver, and the fewer cars on the road, the better. It was a trouble-free journey, and she arrived at her mother's house an hour later. Her mother was all prepared. The grapes and the chocolates and the largest get-well-soon card she could find were all sitting on the table, waiting to go. She had her coat and hat on and was itching to get started.

'Hold on, Mother. I have been driving for an hour. The least you can do is make me a hot drink,'

'Sorry, dear, I am so worried about Graham that I just wasn't thinking. Tea or coffee?'

'Coffee, please. We shan't make the afternoon visiting times, so we have hours to go before we can see him.'

'I do hope he has come out of his coma,' said Grandma Peters.

Mrs Peters hadn't thought for one moment that her son would still be in a coma, but listening to her mother even suggesting that he might not have sent a shiver down her spine. It was 1 p.m. when they left for Portsmouth. They could have made the two-to-four visiting times, but Mrs Peters thought it would be right to let Pam and Graham have a little private time to themselves.

Martin had tried to contact Graham the afternoon before. He also was getting worried, and in desperation, he phoned Portsmouth police station, which confirmed his fears that Graham had been involved in an accident and had been taken to Portsmouth General Hospital. He decided immediately that he would take the next day off and go down to Portsmouth to visit his friend and offer his assistance to Pam. He phoned the chief super and informed him of his intentions. The chief super agreed wholeheartedly that he should go, saying that he was sure he was speaking for the whole force in wishing him a speedy recovery.

He drove down in the morning and arrived at Cedar Ward at 1.30 p.m. The duty nurse was kind enough to let him visit his friend.

'He only woke up a few hours ago, so he will be a bit fragile, so bear that in mind when you speak to him,' she advised him then led him down the ward to Graham's bed.

'I have a visitor for you, Mr Peters,' she said then left them.

'Hello, Martin,' Graham said feebly. 'What are you doing here?'

'I have come to see if you're all right, stupid. What do you think I am doing here? What on earth happened?'

'I don't really know,' said Graham. 'What I can remember is when I left you, I made myself comfortable, I switched the radio on, and drove home. I started to think of the events of the day and how I was going to break the news to my client that her father was a mass killer of children. Or should I even tell her? Would it be better to leave her in ignorance? What if she found out by accident? Can you see my dilemma, Martin?'

'That sure is a problem—you're damned if you do and damned if you don't,' said Martin stroking his chin.

'Anyway, after I had failed to come to any suitable conclusion, my mind drifted to my own problem.'

'What problem is that, Graham?' said Martin in the vain hope he might be able to help Graham for a change.

'Of course I haven't told you, have I? You remember me telling you that I didn't think my nightmares would go until I returned the stolen property back to its rightful family. Well, I was correct in my theory, and they did indeed subside—well almost. I do have one little recurring dream that just won't go away.'

Martin didn't know what it was about Graham and his stories, but he managed to hook him every time. 'Tell me about it, Graham. Maybe I will be able to help you. It is not another murder to solve, is it?'

'No, I am afraid not, Martin. How can I put it? It is like a loose end to the other dream. I think there is one item from the robbery that has not been returned to the Goldsteins, and that is what is cropping up every night in my dreams.'

'Well, come on, don't keep me in suspense, what is it?' asked Martin enthusiastically.

'All it is,' said Graham, 'is a gold locket and chain. I see it very clearly in my dreams. The locket is heart-shaped, and inscribed on the front of it is the word *love*. That is what I was thinking about when I lost concentration. My mind centred on Annie Philpot's grave, and I began to wonder, when you and Dave Harris emptied the contents of the sack on the grass, did you miss it when you gathered it all up again? Then I thought that maybe someone at the station had taken a shine to it, or did Arthur Tidwell drop it when he was being chased along Broad Street? Anyway the point I am about to make is I got so deep into thought that I failed to do what I should have been doing, and that was concentrate on my driving. Hitting the kerb with my wheel soon brought me back to my senses. I tried to correct myself but it was a little too late. The last thing that I remembered was saying hello to a tree.'

'You should have rested in the police station before you left. You had been up all night. You must have been knackered. What on earth were you thinking?' said Martin.

'I know, but don't you start. I will get plenty of that when my wife and mother get here, talking of which, here comes my wife now.'

Pam and her parents gathered around the bed. 'Thank God you have woken up. How is your head, darling?'

Graham put both hands on the sides of his face. 'Thankfully it's still on my shoulders.'

'At least you have still got your sense of humour,' Pam said, sounding as though she had completely lost hers. 'Sorry, Martin—Mum, Dad, this is DCI Martin Penn. If it wasn't for him, I would never have met Graham.'

'I am pleased to meet you both. This son-in-law of yours is the most remarkable man I know. He has solved five murders and a robbery for me, and he is not even a policeman.'

'Don't leave on our account,' said Ben. 'You travelled such a long way to see your friend.'

'No, I understand this should be a family affair, so I will leave you to it.' He wished Graham a quick recovery and said his goodbyes to Pam and her parents then headed back to Hamwell. He didn't know why he did it, but before he returned home, he visited

Annie Philpot's graveside in a vain hope he would stumble across a chain and locket lying in the grass.

Back in Cedar ward, Graham had managed to sit up.

'How is the car, dear? Did they manage to get it home?'

'No. It's probably in the local scrapyard by now. When you do something Graham, you don't do it in half measures.'

'How are you getting about then?' asked Graham.

'I slept at Mum and Dad's last night. It's Sod's Law, isn't it? No sooner do I give up my job to go on maternity leave and sell the car, you write your car off. Never mind, look on the bright side,' she said, directing the remark to herself. 'At least your husband is not a write-off.'

Dr Visram was doing his rounds. He approached Graham's bed and picked up the chart that was hanging on the end of the bed. 'Good, good,' he uttered. 'I can't see any reason why he can't go home tomorrow, Mrs Peters. Just take things easy for a week and definitely no driving.'

'That will not be a problem, Doctor. He has made sure of that,' she said sarcastically.

The time seemed to fly by. The bell rang for the visitors to leave. They said their goodbyes and walked out of the hospital.

'Why don't the both of you go home, and I will hang around until the next visiting time?' Pam suggested to her parents.

'Oh no, you won't, my girl.' It was a rare moment of taking charge of the situation coming from her father. 'This is what we will do—we will all go home, and you can take the car and bring it back at the weekend, and that is final. It will only be sitting on the drive until then.'

'Are you sure, Dad?'

'I have never been surer of anything in my life, so I don't want to hear another word about it.'

'Thanks, Dad. Thanks, Mum. You really are the best mum and dad in the world.'

'Don't be daft, lass, it's what any parent worth their salt would do,'

That evening, she set off once again to see Graham. She arrived a little bit before her mother-in-law, giving herself a little time to speak to her husband before they turned up. She told him about her parents' generosity in letting her use the car and how she couldn't wait to get him home and how she would use the cash she got from selling her car to put down as a deposit on another one. Graham listened but all the visiting was beginning to tire him. The double doors swung open, and Mrs Peters and her mother entered the ward. Grandma Time had arrived.

She made a beeline for Graham's bed. 'You poor boy, how are you? You really must take more care. I have been worried sick.' She reached to her bag and pulled out, first, the chocolates—'Don't scoff them all at once,' she ordered—then the grapes (he had so much fruit on the bedside table it was beginning to look like a greengrocer's shop) then out came the enormous get-well-soon card. It was hard to find a place to position it with all the fruit and chocolates, but Grandma managed to prop it up on top of the chocolate box. Pam and Mrs Peters looked on at this display of lavish affection; they were touched by it but at the same time found it quite amusing. 'I have brought you a book to read. It is a science fiction, something for you to while away the hours. It can get boring lying in bed day in, day out.'

Graham hadn't the heart to tell her that he was being discharged the next day. Instead, he just looked at Pam and his mother and said, 'Isn't that kind of Grandma?' in a way that told them he didn't want them to say that he was being discharged.

They chatted away for the whole of the visiting time. The longer it went on, the harder it became to find things to say. The bell rang to signal the end of visiting time, and the visitors began to vacate the ward. Mrs Peters leaned over and kissed her son goodbye.

Pam kissed him next. 'Sleep well, darling. I wish I could hop in there with you,' she said, flashing her eyes at him.

'So do I,' he said, 'but you might be disappointed because at the moment, all I want to do is sleep.'

Grandma tried to lean over and kiss him goodbye, but her age and lack of flexibility wouldn't allow her to get right over to Graham's face. 'Can you raise your head up and lean over to me just a little, Graham? I am not as young as I used to be,' she complained.

He raised his head and leaned across to meet his Grandma's cheek. He hesitated for a brief moment. He noticed she was wearing something around her neck—it was a gold chain with a heart-shaped locket. Inscribed on the locket were the letters *love*. 'I can't tell you how glad I am that you came to see me today, Grandma.' He then gave her a big kiss. He slumped back on to his pillow, realising that this was his eureka moment. 'Of course,' he muttered, 'it had to be him who took it. Otherwise how the devil would I know it was missing?'

'What was that you just said, darling?' said Pam.

'Nothing, dear. I will tell you tomorrow.'

'Why on earth are you smiling like that?'

'Why shouldn't I smile?' he said. 'I am the happiest man in the world. Good night, dear.'

'Goodnight, darling.' She looked puzzled. 'It must be the drugs and the bang on the head affecting him,' she convinced herself.

CHAPTER TWENTY-TWO

The next morning, Pam went to pick up Graham from hospital. She arrived at 11 a.m., but it was late afternoon before Graham was discharged. Although his head was still a little sore, he felt well enough to walk to the car unassisted. He arrived home to find his mother and Grandma at his house to welcome him. No sooner had he arrived home and sat down than a cup of coffee was placed in front of him. All evening, someone would ask him, 'Are you sure you are all right, Graham?' and all evening, he would reply, 'Yes, I am, now stop worrying.'

Graham's mother was putting up his grandma overnight and at about 9 p.m., she suggested that it was time for them to leave.

'Before you leave, Grandma,' said Graham, 'can I ask you a question?'

'What is it?' she said.

'That locket and chain that you are wearing, can you tell me where you got it from?'

'It is a family heirloom. It was my mother's, and her mother's before that.'

'I thought it might be,' he said. 'I have a nasty feeling that it is part of the contents of the robbery that your grandfather Arthur Tidwell committed when he murdered Mr Goldstein.'

'Oh my god, do you really think so, Graham?'

'Yes I do. My dreams that I was having have all but gone, but there is one recurring one that is still niggling away, and it's a hand holding out a locket and chain, and engraved on the locket is the word *love*, exactly like the one you are wearing. I know I can't make you, Grandma, but I would like you to give it to me so that I might return it back to the Goldsteins and end my torment.'

'Of course you must have it.'

'I will buy you a replacement one.'

'No, you won't. It will only remind me of my evil grandfather, and now I know its gory history, I don't think I want it any more.'

'Thank you, Grandma,'

'Hey, I have just realised something. My search for answers to the meaning of my dreams, Grandma, started and ended with you. Well, it's not quite over, and I do still have some loose ends to tie up.'

'What would they be, Graham?' she asked.

'Well!' Graham sighed a deep sigh. 'First, I have to confront Clare Clarke to explain my actions. I am not relishing the moment when I tell her that her father was a multiple child murderer, and I do hope she will be able to forgive me in time.'

Putting her arm around him, Pam offered her support. 'We are in this together, Graham. I shall come with you, and after all, I was equally complicit in the deception.'

'Thanks, Pam. I think I will need your support.' He leant over and kissed his wife's cheek then sighed again. This time, it was a happier sigh. 'Then of course I must return this locket back to Jeff and Mary Goldstein and hope that will be the end of my troublesome dreams. I am keen to see how their windfall has affected their lives. I do hope they have not wasted it. I am sure if it is left to Mary to take charge of the finances, everything will turn out just fine, but if it is left to Jeff, well!' Graham left his audience to interpret their own conclusion to his thinking.

Graham's mother reassured them by saying, 'Whatever you do, I am sure it will be the right thing to do, but now Grandma and I must head off home.' She always called her mother Grandma in the company of her son, and it seemed so natural somehow.

Four weeks seemed to have flown by since Graham had been discharged from hospital. Pam had been keeping a keen eye on him, and she was now satisfied that he was not suffering any long-lasting effects as a result of his bang on the head, so when he suggested to her that he thought he was well enough to pay Jeff and Mary Goldstein a visit, she offered no objections and suggested that she accompanied him, and afterwards, they could pop into the police station so she could catch up with some of her old friends.

'Why not? I would like to see Martin just to thank him for visiting me in hospital. How about this weekend?' he suggested. 'Also, I am due back to work on Monday, so how about we make it a long weekend and book in at the Ferryman for Friday and Saturday nights? That way, most of the people we want to see at the station should still be working on Friday, and Saturday, we can visit Jeff and Mary. Does that make sense?'

'I like that idea very much, Graham, especially the idea of staying at the Ferryman. It does hold some romantic memories for us.'

'Right, that is settled then. I will book it immediately.' Ten minutes later, their weekend was planned.

Friday morning was one of those dull, gloomy mornings, not really a day for travelling long distances, but it didn't deter them. They finished their breakfast then decided to make an early start for Hamwell. They had invested in a new car the week before, a bright-red Ford Escort. Graham hadn't driven it yet. He hadn't stepped behind the wheel of any vehicle since his accident, but he naturally went to the driver's door.

'Oh, no you don't, young man. You will be in the passenger seat for this journey,' Pam insisted. 'If you are a good boy, I might let you drive for a little way on the way home.'

He gave no objection; in truth, he was a little nervous about getting behind the wheel again.

Pam was somewhat surprised by her husband's lack of protest, which made her feel a little guilty. 'It's for the best, dear, just until your confidence returns.'

'You're right as usual, so let's get going.' He was annoyed but not with her—with himself for being inadequate.

They stopped halfway, at a motorway service station. It was there that they decided to make their first visit, the police station. After a hot drink and a sandwich, they set off again and arrived at Hamwell police station at 1.45 p.m. Entering the front door, the first person they bumped into was Chief Superintendent Ronald Hawkins. He was busy posting the previous month's detection figures on the noticeboard. He turned around to see who was standing behind him. His face immediately lit up. 'Pam, Graham, how nice to see you. I trust you're both well. What brings you this way? Do you have another juicy mystery to solve? I do hope so,' he said, rubbing his hands together in glee.

'No such luck, sir,' said Pam. 'This is just a social visit to catch up with old pals.'

'Well, feel free to use the canteen, and if you get any more ghosts coming out of the closet, remember us, won't you? I will leave a note on Martin's desk. I am sure he will be delighted to see you both.'

They thanked the chief and made their way to the canteen, where they sat all afternoon. Pam's old colleagues drifted in one by one. Everyone, without exception, seemed delighted to see her and she them. They discussed all that had happened since she had left the station, who was going out with who. Some were very interested in her participation in the locating of four children that had been murdered by Clarke. She enjoyed telling them the intimate details and seeing them mesmerised as she had been mesmerised by Graham's account of his experience with his dreams. Every time she was asked to recite the events, she always ended with telling her audience that the children would still be lying there if it hadn't been for the brilliant mind of the man sitting beside her. Graham was quite happy to sit there while she impressed her colleagues; however, he was waiting to see Martin, although it seemed more and more likely that he was not going to make an appearance. The chief walked into the canteen; he seemed surprised that they were still there.

'Martin phoned in a short while ago. He is held up on a case, and he asked me to ask you if you are staying in Hamwell overnight, and if you are, where, and if so, to leave your address on his desk and he will catch up with you both later.'

Graham wrote the name of the Ferryman Hotel on a piece of paper and handed it to the chief. 'I suppose we had better go and get booked in at the hotel then, Pam—that is, if you have seen everyone.'

Pam's back was beginning to pain her, what with her sitting so long and being seven months pregnant.

'That sounds good to me, dear,' she groaned, trying hard not to show the discomfort that she was in. They said their goodbyes to the chief and made their way to the Ferryman. After booking in, they made their way to their room. Pam took one look at the bed and plonked herself down. By the time Graham had emptied the suitcases, she was dead to the world. He made himself a hot drink and sat quietly on one of the two armchairs in the room. His mind began to drift back to the last time he had been there and all the events that had transpired since then. After churning over all that had happened, he said to himself, 'Arthur Tidwell, you sure led me a merry dance.' He turned his head around and looked at his wife sleeping peacefully then got up from his chair and slid in beside her, and that is where they stayed for the next two hours. They were awoken by the phone ringing. Graham reached over to pick it up.

'Reception here, sir. I have a gentleman here asking for you. Are you available to see him?'

'Yes.' He knew immediately it was Martin. 'Please ask him to wait and tell him I will be with him in ten minutes.'

'What is it?' said Pam, still half asleep.

'Martin is downstairs,'

'You go down, Graham, and I will follow as soon as I am dressed.'

Graham hadn't bothered to undress before he slipped into bed, so he shot into the bathroom, cleaned his teeth, wiped a flannel over his face, and ran a comb through his hair, and away he went to meet his friend. Their greeting was exceptionally warm, considering how strange their first encounter was. They had both served each other well in the past, and a bond of respect for each other had built up between them, and it had developed into a strong friendship.

'Where is Pam?' Martin enquired.

'You caught us both having forty winks, but she will be down shortly. She is seven months pregnant now, and the strain is beginning to tell, but I know she would love to see you, so I hope you can stay long enough until she shows. In the meantime, let me buy you a drink.'

'Oh, no you don't, young man. It is high time I bought you one. I don't think you are aware of how pulling a young man out of a grave has changed my career for the better. Let me tell you something, Graham—I have been promoted, and I now give lectures to young rookie detectives, and one of the lessons that I try to teach them is always listen to the person you are interviewing at the other side of the table. Then I go into detail about my experience with you, and it captures their interest every single time.'

Graham looked quite taken aback by his friend's openness and sincerity and, for a moment, was lost for words.

'Sorry, Graham, I have embarrassed you,' Martin said apologetically.

'No, no, not at all. I am pleased that some positives are coming out of what, for me, has been a very stressful time in my life. In fact, when you think about it, nothing but good has come from it.'

'What do you mean?' said Martin, somewhat puzzled.

'Well, think about it—your promotion and the material that it has provided for your lectures and me meeting Pam.'

Martin interrupted, 'Don't forget the gold that you recovered that has made the Goldsteins' life so much richer.'

'That is right,' said Graham, 'and then there is the solving of Mr Goldstein's murder.'

They started to bounce off each other. 'Then there is the discovery of the poor children on the island at the lake. We would never have found them without you, Graham.'

'That is right, and think of the parents of the children and how relieved they must be that they can at last put to rest their agony of not knowing what happened to them.'

'After I left you at the hospital, I took a little detour on the way home. I checked out Annie Philpot's grave to see if I could find the gold chain that you were telling me about. Without success, I might add.'

'Thanks, Martin, but I have found it. In fact, that is the other reason that we are here, to return it to the Goldsteins.'

'Where on earth did you find it?' said Martin, genuinely astonished.

'It was hanging around my grandmother's neck. Arthur Tidwell must have taken a shine to it, and gave it to his wife, and it has been handed down as an heirloom ever since.'

Martin was just about to say that Graham should get all his experiences written down, when he saw Pam enter the lounge.

'Well, young lady, you're looking very—'

Pam stopped him before he could finish his sentence. '*Fat*, I think, is the word that you are looking for.' As much as she wanted a baby, feeling and looking like a beached whale was not exactly filling her with the joys of spring.

'I was about to say that you were looking rather mumsy—it was meant to be a compliment.'

She walked straight over to him and kissed his cheek. 'Sorry Martin, how are you? And please forgive me for being a little tetchy, but it isn't easy carrying this load around day in and day out.'

'Apology accepted, now sit down and let me buy both of you a drink. Pam, what would you like?'

'Just a nice hot cup of tea for me, please.' The thought of alcohol turned her stomach over.

'Okay, and you, Graham?'

'Mine is a pint of lager please.'

Martin went to the bar and left them both sitting there.

'Is everything all right, Pam?' Graham enquired, noticing how sharp she had been with Martin.

'Yes, I am fine, dear. Perhaps I am a bit disappointed that the magic of the last time we were here is missing this time, and before you say "Don't you love me any more?" yes, I do—it is just this great lump that I am carrying has taken the shine off of the weekend.'

He gave her hand a squeeze, saying, 'It's not long now, dear, just two more months. I expect you would prefer to be sitting in the comfort of our own home now, wouldn't you?'

'Yes, I would, dear,'

'We will check out early tomorrow, then go straight round to Jeff and Mary's, then go home.'

'Thanks, Graham. I am sorry that I have ruined your weekend.'

Before he could offer her a few more words of comfort, Martin returned with the drinks. He sat down, and they began to chat again. Martin's phone rang. 'Sorry, dear, I completely forgot. I will be home in fifteen minutes.' He looked at Graham and Pam. 'That was the wife,' he said guiltily. 'I completely forgot that she asked me to get home early. Her parents are coming for the weekend, and she is expecting me to pick them up at the station. I might just have time if I leave now.' He apologised to them and took one large gulp of his beer and rushed out of the door.

Pam was relieved he had left early but never conveyed her feelings to her husband. But if she had, he would have told her that he was also relieved.

'Let us order dinner and have it sent to our room,' he suggested, knowing how uncomfortable she felt in public, in her condition.

'Thanks, dear,'

Her resigned reply told him that the day had caught up with her and no less than an early night would fulfil her needs.

The following morning, it was Graham who rose first. He pulled back the curtains; the rain was teeming down. Pam opened her eyes and yawned. 'What are you looking at, Graham?' She spoke in a voice that sounded as though it hadn't woken up yet.

'Good morning, my love.' He walked to the bedside and leaned over and kissed her forehead. 'I was looking out at the weather. It is hammering down out there. Anyway, how are you feeling this morning?'

'A lot better than last night, I am relieved to say.'

'Good. I will make you a coffee, then we can go down and have a light breakfast, then go and give Jeff and Mary the locket, then head for home.'

They checked out of the hotel at just before 10 a.m. and made their way to the Goldsteins' house. Pulling up outside, they noticed that a block paving driveway had been laid, and a small hatchback car was sitting on it. A Lambretta-type scooter stood to one side of the car. A new shiny green front door and double-glazed windows gave the house a real cared-for look. They sat in the car for a moment, wondering whether Jeff and Mary had moved house or if they had put their newfound fortune to good use. Knocking on the door, they quite expected a complete stranger to open it.

'Graham, Pam, how wonderful, please come in.' Mary's face expressed beautifully her delight at seeing them. 'Jeff will be delighted. He is always talking about you, wondering what you are both doing now. Come in, he is playing with the twins.' She led them to the front room door then, before she opened it, turned around to face them then put a finger across her lips, whispering to them to be quiet, then entered the room. 'There are two people here to see you, Jeff. Shall I bring them in out of the rain?'

'Of course, Mary. Okay, kids, playtime is over.'

Mary beckoned them in.

Jeff jumped up from the floor. 'Graham, mate, I was talking about you only the other day, and Pam, how are you?' He looked down at her swollen tummy and added, 'That was a silly question, wasn't it?'

'Please sit down, and I will make some tea,' said Mary, clearing the children's toys off the settee. They seated themselves down. Graham couldn't help but notice the difference in the quality of their furnishings compared to the last time that he had sat on the sofa in that room. It gave him a good feeling, knowing that none of the improvements that they had made would have been possible without him discovering the meaning of his dreams. The four of them sat chatting for an hour. Mary told them that they were no longer renting their property and how she had passed her driving test and what a relief it was not walking the children to the supermarket in the pushchair anymore.

Jeff said he had a job working in a warehouse and how he used his scooter to get back and forth.

Do You Believe in Life After Death?

After they had exhausted all the conversation, Graham came to the point of his visit. He started by telling them that after he returned the stolen loot back to them, he still had a dream about a locket with the word *love* engraved on it and how he assumed it was part of the robbery that hadn't been returned with the rest of the robbery proceeds. Then he told them how he found it, purely by accident, hanging around his grandmother's neck and how she told him it was a heirloom passed down through the generations and, by putting two and two together, how he had worked out that his notorious great-great-grandfather must have taken a shine to it and presented it to his wife.

'Crikey, mate, you sure are a clever sod, aren't you?' said Jeff.

'Language, Jeff,' said Mary.

'Sorry, dear.'

'Anyway,' continued Graham, 'I have brought it with me and want to return it to you today.'

Mary interrupted, 'You didn't have to come all that way just to hand us an old locket. Honestly, you have both done more for us than we could ever repay you for.'

'You don't understand, Mary. I am not doing this for you. I am doing it for me. I am hoping that by me presenting you with the locket, it will free me of all the bad dreams and allow my troubled ancestor to rest in peace.'

'You're not going to have one of your spooky moments again, are you, Graham?' said Jeff, remembering the last time he presented them with loot from the robbery. 'I don't mind telling you it scared me witless.'

The three of them all laughed at his remark, then Graham put his arms out in front of him, imitating a ghost. 'I am coming for you, Jeffrey Goldstein.' He made Jeff take a step backwards; the look on his face made the two women burst their sides with laughter.

177

'You can be a real wimp at times, Jeff,' said Mary, while at the same time trying to control her laughter.

'No, Jeff is quite right. I didn't know what would happen then, and I don't know what will happen now. What I do know is that it has to be done.'

The mood changed immediately from a jovial atmosphere to one of complete solemnity. A few moments of silence were finally broken by Pam. 'There is no time like the present,' she uttered rather nervously. 'Is that okay with Jeff?'

'If we have to, but I don't like it.'

'And you, Mary?'

'I am fine with it. It's like four people sitting around a table at a séance, and I think it is quite exciting.'

Graham took a deep breath then reached into his pocket for the locket and chain. They all stared at his hand as though they were expecting something sinister to appear, like a hand grenade or a dagger or something equally threatening.

Graham thought it best to use the same approach to the handover this time as he had the first time at the police station. 'Jeff, on behalf of myself and my deceased relative Arthur Tidwell, may I return what I believe to be the last item of the robbery committed by him all those years ago and say sorry once again for all the pain that his thoughtless act has caused you.' Again, Graham's voice changed when he said he was sorry, but he didn't collapse. He broke down and sobbed uncontrollably for the best part of three minutes.

Pam and Mary comforted him by putting their arms around him. 'That's right,' said Pam, 'let it all out. Let Jeff and Mary see how truly sorry Arthur is for his actions.'

He wiped his eyes and looked sorrowfully up at Jeff, who was standing directly in front of him. He could see the remorse quite clearly on Graham's sad face and, in words that only Jeff could speak in a situation such as the one he had just witnessed, uttered, 'Jesus, mate, your dead relative has really screwed you up, hasn't he?'

'I couldn't have put it better myself,' said Graham, rustling up a smidgen of humour. 'I really am sorry that I made you go through it all again, but it had to be done to exorcise my demons. You do see that, don't you?'

'Of course we do,' replied Mary. 'You have done so much for us, helping us to get back on our feet again, that any small thing we can do to relieve your torment is the least we can do for you.'

'That's dead right,' said Jeff. 'It is about time we did something for you, so let us treat you to lunch before you return home. That is, of course, if you feel like it.'

'That is very nice of you, Jeff,' said Pam. 'Do you think you will have recovered enough to eat, dear?'

'Why not?' he replied. 'I think we have something to celebrate, don't you?'

An hour later, Graham was back to his normal self again, upbeat about the conclusion of his mental journey and beginning to feel quite peckish. However, all Pam wanted was to get in the car and drive home but, not wanting to upset anybody, decided to keep quiet and go along with the Goldsteins' wish to pay back a little of the generosity that Graham had given them. It was 2 p.m. before they finally returned back to the Goldsteins' house. They didn't go inside, and instead, they said their goodbyes in the car, explaining that Pam was feeling rather tired. Mary sympathised, remembering the agony of carrying the twins around for nine months, and it was not something she wanted to repeat again in a hurry, so she was fully aware of the discomfort poor Pam was experiencing.

'I do understand, Pam. You must let us know when the baby arrives. Now you get off home,' she ordered, sounding like a mother hen.

They drove away, and within minutes, Pam was fast asleep, and that was the way she stayed until Graham pulled into their driveway. 'We are home, dear,' he whispered.

'Home sweet home, how good that sounds,' she sighed. 'Can I leave you to bring the suitcase in, Graham? I afraid that I am all in.'

He leaned over and kissed her cheek. 'Of course, dear. It has been a bit of an ordeal for you, hasn't it?'

'You can say that again.'

He took the cases out of the car and left them in the hallway, deciding to make his wife a hot drink first, but he was too late. She was already in bed, fast asleep.

CHAPTER TWENTY-THREE

Two months had raced by since their visit to Hamwell. The phone rang. It was Jeff, enquiring whether there was any news on the baby. Both he and Mary were also eager to know whether Graham had exorcised his demons. With sheer delight, Graham reported that he hadn't been visited once by his dead relative since handing back the locket to them and was sleeping like a baby every night.

'That is fantastic,' said Jeff. 'I am pleased that we had a small part in it.'

'So am I, Jeff, so am I,' said Graham. It got him thinking yet again how one mindless act such a long time ago can bring two families together in friendship over a hundred years later.

'I am handing the phone over to Mary now. She wants an update on Pam's condition, so good luck, mate, and keep in touch.'

'Hello, Graham, I was listening to your conversation with Jeff, and that is such good news about your dreams—or should I say lack of them. Is Pam available to come to the phone?'

'Thanks Mary. Pam, it's Mary on the phone. She wants to speak with you.'

'Hello, Mary, how are you?'

'I am fine. How are you? Not long now, I would imagine?'

'It feels like it will arrive at any minute. Oh, to slip into a dress and look in the mirror and like what I see.'

'I remember the feeling so well,' said Mary, casting her mind back to the weeks before the twins were born.

They chatted on the phone for another half an hour before Pam's back ached so bad that she was forced to say her goodbyes.

Professor Irvin sat eating a corned-beef-and-tomato sandwich at his desk when the phone rang.

'Mrs Peters, how are you?'

'Very well, thank you, Professor, and you?'

'I am fine, thank you. Do you want to speak to your son?'

'No, but could you pass a message to him?'

'Yes, of course, what is it?'

'He always said he would like to be present at the birth of his child, so if he is not home in the next four hours, there is a good chance he will miss it.'

'Holy Moses, message received and understood. I will tell him straight away, oh! Premature congratulations, Mrs Peters.' He then put the phone down, took one large bite out of his sandwich, and shot out of his office and into the laboratory, heading towards Graham.

Graham turned towards the slightly flustered professor. 'Are you all right, sir?' he enquired, having never seen him even slightly flustered before.

'Go home, Graham. Go home now, or you will miss the birth of your first child.'

'But, sir, what about my work?'

'That will still be here tomorrow. Now if you are still here in five minutes, I will fire you, so off you go.'

'Thanks, Professor, I will phone you later and let you know how it went.' And with that, he took off his white laboratory coat and rushed out of the building.

Graham's front door was open when he arrived home. He noticed two unfamiliar cars parked outside. He assumed one was the doctor's and the other the midwife's. He was greeted by his mother and Pam's parents. All three of them were showing the signs of concern that parents show when one of their children is in pain.

'Is everything all right?' Graham asked gingerly.

'As far as we are aware,' said Ben, 'it won't be long now, but we think it would be a good idea if you went straight up to comfort her.'

He gave all three of them a glancing look as though to seek their approval before going to his wife, then ran up the stairs to Pam. On entering the bedroom, he could hear the midwife giving her instructions, telling Pam to push. The doctor was observing.

'Is it all right to come in?' Graham asked softly.

The doctor turned around. 'Mr Peters, yes, come in. It won't be long now, and everything is going fine. Your wife is a good patient. Why don't you hold her hand?'

He walked to the opposite side of the bed to where the doctor was standing then took Pam's hand at just the moment she was having a painful contraction.

'That's good, keep pushing,' instructed the midwife. Graham wiped her brow and tried to comfort her by whispering, 'I am here now, dear.'

'Don't you ever come near me again,' she screamed.

Graham looked up at the doctor as if to say 'What did I do?'

'One last push, Mrs Peters! Good, keep pushing, well done! Could you please hand me a towel, Doctor? Mr Peters, your wife has just presented you with a beautiful son,' she proudly announced.

She handed the child to him and suggested that he put the baby in his mother's arms.

Before handing his new son to its mother, he took a moment to look at the marvel that he was holding. This was his son, a wonder of nature, so beautiful, and he felt quite humbled by the gift that his wife had presented him with. A little cry made him return from the wonderment of the moment. he gently leaned over and handed the little bundle over to his wife. With his voice full of emotion, he uttered, 'He is beautiful, Pam. Thank you for the best gift a man could possibly receive from his wife.'

Pam took her newborn and studied him. 'He's perfect, isn't he? Look at his little fingers and toes—they are so small.' They both marvelled at their new creation for a good fifteen minutes before Pam looked up.

'Nurse?'

'Yes, Mrs Peters?'

'Would it be all right for our parents to come up and see the baby? They must be champing at the bit waiting downstairs.'

'I think that will be okay. Just give me a minute to pack up my things and get out of your way.'

She made her appointment for her follow-up visit, then they both thanked her for all she had done.

'I will tell your parents it is all clear to come up on my way out.'

They didn't need telling twice. They went up the stairs like rats up a drainpipe. Graham stood back and let the mothers have their moment; Ben stood back with his son-in-law. 'Have you decided on a name yet, Graham?' he asked.

'Yes, we have—Benjamin in honour of you, Ben, and Martin as a second name in honour of the DCI that brought us both together and has become a great friend to me.'

'Ben Peters—yes, I like it. Thanks, Graham, I do feel honoured. Look, let's leave the ladies to it and go and wet the baby's head.'

'That sounds good to me, Ben. We had better tell the ladies where we are going.'

He informed the mothers that he and Ben were off for a pint, but for all the notice they took, he might just as well have said it in Chinese.

'Come on, Ben, let's leave them to it.'

The following few months seemed to fly by. Parenthood was demanding but rewarding. Baby Ben's hair had grown, and he began to sit up by himself. Life was good for the Peterses. It was on one night when Graham was bouncing Ben on his lap that he cast his mind back to his troublesome days. It reminded him of Jeff doing the very same thing with the twins, and that led him to thinking about Clare and the fact that they had not contacted her since the discovery of the children that her father had murdered in his desire for some sick, perverted sexual need to be catered for. She, on the other hand, had not bothered contacting them either. Was she aware of the discovery? Had she put two and two together? Had her bad dreams vanished? Could she now find friendship with the opposite sex? The more he thought about it, the more his curiosity grew.

Pam entered the room; she looked across at where Graham was sitting. 'A penny for your thoughts dear?' she uttered, noticing although he was playing with his son, his mind was somewhere else.

'I was thinking about Clare Clarke and wondering how she was doing. It is strange, the fact we have not heard from her since the last time we saw her. I do hope she is all right.'

'I had completely forgotten about her,' Pam replied. 'I wonder if her disturbing dreams have vanished?'

'I was thinking the very same thing. If my theory was right, then yes, they have, but I would like to know for certain.'

'Why don't we pay her a surprise visit next weekend, Graham? It will give us an excuse to show off baby Ben to her?'

'Putting it like that, how can I refuse? Shall we say Sunday?'

'Sunday it is, Daddy' she agreed.

He lifted his son up. 'Did you hear that, Ben? Mummy is going to show you off?'

Pam took Ben off Graham's lap to give him his evening feed, which left Graham to slip into his thought mode once again. The more he thought about Clare's noncommunication with them, the more unsettled he was becoming that something might be wrong. The feeling grew and grew until the morning that they had planned to go and see her; by then, he couldn't get it out of his mind.

Pam had dressed Ben in her favourite little denim suit. Graham opened the car door, while Pam strapped Ben into the baby car seat. When she had finished, she sat in the front passenger seat next to her husband.

Graham checked with her that she was ready to travel, then looked back at Ben looking quite dapper in his denim suit. 'How about you, Elvis? Are you ready to rock? Well, come on then, let us roll!'

They arrived outside Clare's house just before midday. A car was parked directly outside the front gate. It was one of those half cars—as Pam liked to call them—all front and no back. For some unknown reason, Graham started to feel very nervous. Pam took Ben out of his chair and ran a comb through his hair to make sure he looked his best when meeting Clare.

They were about to get out of the car when Clare's front door opened. A man in his late forties to early fifties came out and disappeared around the side of the house, only to reappear wheeling a bike. He stopped by the front door and shouted back, 'I am off now, darling. I will see you later.'

Clare appeared. She put her arms around him and kissed him goodbye, and he then cycled off, passing straight by them without even noticing that they were there.

They gave him a couple of minutes to disappear then got out of the car and walked up to Clare's front door. They rang the bell and prepared themselves for a happy reunion. The door opened, and the sight of them made her happy expression drop like a stone.

'You two have got a bloody nerve coming here' was her opening salvo.

They stood stunned by what they had just heard, then Graham pulled himself together and asked, 'What's wrong, Clare? What on earth have we done?'

'What have you done? I will tell you what you have done. First you cart me around god knows how many lakes on the pretence that you were helping me understand my dreams, while the real reason you conveniently kept from me. I thought you to be my friends. How wrong was I.'

'There was a good reason for not telling you the whole truth, Clare, and that was the content of your dreams, in my opinion, revealed something very sinister, and if I were to get to the bottom of them, I felt telling you my suspicions would only get in the way of my experiment.'

'Oh I was a bloody experiment, now was I? Well, isn't that just hunky-dory? Oh, and thank you for informing the police about me. I can't tell you how pleased I was to have them knocking on my door wanting to know my life story,'

'I didn't know that, Clare, but let me say this—even though they asked me where I got my information from, it was not me that gave them your name, but taking the gravity of your father's crimes, it was hardly surprising that they paid you a visit.'

Pam's temper was building up like a pressure cooker. This blinkered woman standing in front of her whom they had tried to help was now treating her husband with an illogical disrespect, which he certainly didn't deserve, and to crown it all, she hadn't noticed baby Ben at all. She held her tongue and let Clare finish.

'I apologise for any distress I have caused you, Clare, but can I ask you just one question—are you still having your terrible dreams?'

'No, Graham, that is the only good thing to come out of my association with you two.'

That had done it; Pam's pressure cooker finally exploded.

'The only good thing to come out of associating with us, is it? Well, let me enlighten you to some other things your narrow little mind might not have considered. First, it was you who contacted Graham for help to understand your dreams, and if I remember rightly, he did warn you that whatever he found might not be nice. Yes, we kept the unpalatable truth from you, but what you told us about your dreams and your father's relationship with you made us both feel extremely uneasy. The fact that the dreams featured a man rowing children across a lake, we felt, was so disturbing that we contacted a police officer that we knew to look into missing children who lived in the same location where you once lived. When he came back with the information that we were both dreading, that is when Graham decided that you were the only one who held the key to where your father had buried them. You see, Clare, your father died full of guilt and self-loathing, and he passed all that guilt to you through his DNA, and that is what we tried to unlock when we took you around the lakes. And that feeling of déjà vu that you experienced at the lake was the same as Graham experienced when he investigated his own relative's sordid past.'

Graham stood speechless as his wife fired on both barrels.

'You say no good has come from knowing us. Well, let me list you a few you might have overlooked. When we first met, you had a mental block, which made it impossible for you to strike up a relationship with a member of the opposite sex, but by the way you just said goodbye to that man who came out of your house, I would say that that is another good thing that has come from your association with us, and let's not forget four families living in torment for over forty years not knowing what had happened to their children. Now they have closure, thanks to you, me, and Graham. I think that was a great deal of good that came out of your association with us, don't you?'

'Okay, Pam, you have made your point,' said Graham. Although he agreed with everything his wife said, he didn't like confrontation and felt a little bit sorry for Clare, who could do no more than just stand there and take it. In his usual calm, logical way, he said that they had come to see her in good faith and hoped that one day, she would see that what they had done was the right thing to do and, in time, perhaps become friends again. He apologised once again for any stress that he had caused then turned to his wife, saying, 'Come on, darling, let's go home.'

Graham went into the driver's seat, and Pam strapped Ben into his car seat then got into the front passenger seat, almost slamming the door off its hinges. She was still shaking with rage. 'Let's get as far away from here, as quickly as we can.' Her voice was croaking with rage. 'I don't think she even noticed Ben, and that was unforgivable.'

'It was interesting, though, don't you think, that she no longer has her bad dreams and also that she can, at last, now have a relationship with a man?'

'I couldn't care less about her dreams or about the men in her life. Christ, Graham, what have you got running through your veins, antifreeze?'

'Perhaps it's because I still see her as an experiment, that makes me seem cold, but I can see she has got right under your skin. Although I do find you extremely attractive when you're red-faced and angry, please try and calm down, dear.'

She took a deep breath, smiled at him, and said, 'Come on, you old smoothie, take me home.'

'Your wish is my command, Your Angriness,' he joked.

'Idiot.'

CHAPTER TWENTY-FOUR

Three years had passed, and Graham didn't need to prove his theories any more. He was quite certain that everything that he had uncovered was the absolute truth. His last encounter with Clare had made his mind up that no further good would come from continuing to prove his theories. His home life could not be better. Pam was expecting their second child, and a recent ultrasound confirmed that young Ben would soon be having a sister to play with. The grandparents were delighted with the news. Granddad Ben adored taking his grandson out for the day, and they normally headed for the seafront. Rose accompanied them on the odd occasion, but she preferred to be around her daughter, so losing the boys for the day never worried her in the slightest. Graham's grandma was becoming a little feebler year by year. His mother suggested she sell her house and move in with her, but the stubborn old lady loved her independence and wouldn't hear of it, which meant her daughter had to travel to see her more often than she desired.

Professor Irvin entered the laboratory canteen. He picked up a tray and slid it along the tray rail. He studied the meals on display.

It was a toss-up: curry and rice, sausage and mash, a large portion of ham-and-egg pie with salad or lasagne. After much deliberation, the ham-and-egg pie won the day. He turned around and scanned the canteen for a place to sit. Every table had at least one person sitting at it, and he noticed the table that Graham was sitting at had a spare chair, so he made a beeline for that.

Graham was eating with one hand and writing on a notepad with the other. The words 'Do you mind if I join you, Graham?' made him look up.

'Of course not, Professor. Please sit down,' he replied, at the same time folding up the piece of paper that he had been jotting notes on and slipping it in his pocket.

'Anything interesting?' asked the professor.

'I was just jotting down a few notes regarding my dream experiences.'

'For what purpose?' enquired the professor.

'I thought it was about time I published a paper on it before I forget.'

A large lump of ham-and-egg pie disappeared into the professor's mouth. It took about half a minute before he could speak again. Gulping and pointing his fork at Graham, he offered his assistance.

'Why, yes, that would be most welcome, sir. In truth, I am at a bit of a loss knowing how to start it.'

'Stick to the facts, my boy, just the facts.'

'You are right, Professor—that is what I will do, and when it is finished, perhaps you could run your professional eye over it and give it your seal of approval?'

'I will look forward to that, my boy.' He sliced off another chunk of ham-and-egg pie and, before it entered his mouth, looked at it and said, 'My god, this pie is good.'

'Looking at the way that you are tucking into it is making me wish I chose it for myself.'

Graham worked tirelessly in his spare time recalling the events, putting it all into print, reading it back to himself, and more often than not, screwing it up and starting again. When he had collated all his experiences and felt satisfied that he hadn't missed any of the vital information, only then did he feel confident enough to offer it to the professor for his approval. Two months had elapsed since the professor had spoken to Graham offering his help and advice with his paper. He had submitted three papers himself to the scientific elite for their approval and was acutely aware of what was acceptable and what wasn't.

Graham printed out a spare copy of the finished paper. He put it in a folder and took it into work the following morning. He knocked on the professor's door then entered.

'Is that what I think it is, Graham?' he said.

'That is correct, sir,' came the reply.

'Okay, leave it with me, and I will take it home this weekend. I have to say that I am looking forward to reading it.'

'I want an honest appraisal, sir. If you think it's a load of rubbish, I want you to be straight with me.'

'Don't worry on that score, young man. I have had a little experience submitting papers to my peers for approval, and believe me, if they don't like what they are confronted with, they will reject it quicker than you can say *Jack Robinson*.'

Saturday morning was Mouse's shopping day. She not only shopped for herself, but also for her elderly mother. Although she still lived on her own, she was becoming more and more reliant on her daughter to maintain her independence. She had had a hip replacement two years previously, but at eighty-seven, she found it hard to get about without the aid of a walking stick. Mouse had suggested she think seriously about retiring to a nursing home. If she did, she would be guaranteed twenty-four-hour care and have people her own age to talk to. She had thought about it, but she had lived in her house for sixty-two years, and it held a lot of memories for her—a few bad ones but mainly good. Her daughter always stayed with her on Saturday afternoons. Mouse would put her shopping away for her while she made the tea, and then they would sit and talk. At 4 p.m. on the dot, Mouse would say, 'Just look at the time, Mum. I really must be going.' She felt 4 p.m. was an acceptable time to leave her mother without feeling riddled with guilt.

Professor Irvin cleared up the breakfast plates then poured himself another cup of coffee. Before sitting down, he went to his briefcase and withdrew Graham's papers.

Graham had started by explaining that in order for thought transference to be possible, certain conditions had to be present. First, the donor had to have died bearing a terrible secret that gave him or her extreme guilt and remorse. In order for that guilt and remorse to be transferred to the next generation, the donor had to father or, in the case of a woman, conceive a child whilst experiencing his or her torment. This was how the transfer was made possible through the DNA.

The professor read it back to himself. 'Good, that's right, Graham, stick to the facts.' He continued to read.

> The information handed down may or may not surface in the next generation. Indeed, in my case, it lay dormant for four generations before it surfaced. It appeared in the form of a recurring dream or nightmare. The dreams were trying to tell me to put right the wrong that my ancestor had committed, although I wasn't aware of that at the time. But the more information that I uncovered, the more I felt that the only way to rid myself of the torment was to unravel my dreams and seek out the family that he had wronged and to apologise. There was

a bonus of a great deal of gold which my ancestor had stolen from them. In my search for the truth, I felt strong feelings of déjà vu when visiting the places where my ancestor had committed his crimes.

When I eventually unravelled the mystery and was in a position to confront the wronged family with the facts, a strange thing happened. Whilst giving my apology, my natural speaking voice changed, and the voice that I can only assume was my long-since-deceased relative took over. My dreams decreased in intensity, but one item of the stolen goods had not been returned, and this item bothered my dreams. I believe it was my ancestor once again, who was trying to tell me through his DNA that lived inside me, to finish the task that he had set me in order for him and me to rest in peace. By chance, I found the one remaining item and returned it to the family that he stole it from; once again, my voice changed when I returned it.

In conclusion, I no longer experience haunting dreams. I was interested, however, to know whether my experience was a one-off. If my theories were to be proven beyond any shadow of doubt, then I had to try and find somebody else who was experiencing the same nightmares as I. So I put an advert in three daily papers. It took a considerable length of time before I received a response. A woman in her forties contacted me, saying she was having recurring dreams that were very stressful; they consisted of a man rowing children to an island on a lake. This interested me, and after a lot of sensitive delving into her past, I discovered that her father abused her as a child. This worried me even more. All the conditions for thought transference were emerging. Could it be that her father was abusing other children before she was born, and had he been so riddled with guilt and self-loathing? I asked myself, Was his torment strong enough to pass it to his daughter through his DNA? It also emerged that he had drowned in a lake. There was no reason at the time to suspect foul play, but as I learned more about him, I now suspect he committed suicide, feeling unable to live with his guilt.

I contacted a police detective, DCI Martin Penn, and without telling him why, I asked him to check to see if any children were reported missing in the area where the family had lived from the ten years before his daughter was born. The answer I received filled me with horror: four children had disappeared and had never been found. Again playing a hunch, I asked him if he could check all the lakes with islands in the area where the woman's father had lived. He passed the information to a detective in that area, but they didn't have the manpower to search the considerable amount of lakes involved. That left me with just one other option—that was to try and locate it myself.

An idea came into my head, and it was one that I had experienced in my quest for answers to my own problems—déjà vu. If I could persuade the woman to visit the lakes around the area that she grew up in, it might trigger a response from her subconscious that she had inherited from her father. Of course, I couldn't tell her the real reason, (a) because it might cloud her mind with negative thoughts and (b) she might have refused to participate in my experiment. That weekend, we visited many lakes without success, but eventually, we arrived at one that, in her words, gave her a horrible feeling. Déjà vu had done its job.

The next day, I phoned DCI Penn and told him that I thought I had located the lake where the missing children might be buried. You might recall it—the press headlined it as the Crowley child murders, the miracle find. I feel that my conclusions go a long way to answer the phenomenon that we know as déjà vu. That is the feeling that we have been there before. Could these also be thoughts handed down by the DNA of past generations? I strongly believe this to be so. None of the above would have been possible without thought transference from the dead to the living, a kind of life after death.

I submit my findings to you for scrutiny. Thank you.

The professor returned the paperback into its folder, saying to himself, 'Good, you seem to have covered all the relevant facts.' He then made a couple of notes and returned it into its folder.

Monday morning, and the professor was sitting in his office waiting for Graham to come in. He had left his door open so as to catch sight of him walking by. Graham automatically glanced into the professor's office just to say good morning, but this morning, the professor beckoned him in. 'Take a seat, Graham. I read your paper over the weekend. I think you have set out your theories well. I will pick up on two aspects of it, one positive and one negative. I will give you the negative first—names. The people who will be reading this are not interested in names, so change *DCI Martin Penn* to *the police.*'

'Thank you, Professor. I can do that.'

'The other thing is your link between thought transference and déjà vu. I must say that I, for one, never picked up on the link to thought transference. But you are right—the possibility of a link must be considered. Well done.'

CHAPTER TWENTY-FIVE

Although they had been going to name their daughter after Clare Clarke, their last encounter with her changed their minds, and after many hours of throwing names into the hat and not wanting to offend any of the grandmothers if it was not their name chosen, they eventually opted for Pamela.

Professor Graham Peters now heads the research laboratory after his good friend Professor Irvin recommended his prodigy to step into his boots upon his retirement.

Martin spends most of his time teaching detection skills to young rookie detectives. He still keeps in touch with his good friends Graham and Pam, and he still hopes that he will get another phone call asking him to look into some weird unexplainable event. He lives in hope.

Mary and Pam have become very good friends. They meet up three or four times a year for a girls' day out, swapping stories about the past, reminiscing on the reaction that Jeff had when Graham handed back the locket—that always gives them a good laugh.

Arthur Tidwell, in his senseless act of cruelty all those many years ago, could not have imagined in his wildest dreams how he would affect so many lives over one hundred years later, and all for the good.

ABOUT THE AUTHOR

I am seventy-three years old, married to Kitty for fifty-five years this year, our emerald anniversary. We have two children, Andre and Anita, and four grandchildren—Andre has two, Sophie and Francis; Anita has two, James and Amy.

I was a war baby from a poor background, which meant my education was rather basic, but I have learnt a lot through the school of life. My hobbies are golf, archery, and recently, writing, which I thoroughly enjoy; I wish I had taken it up earlier. Kitty has been a great help with my writings and has furnished me with some good ideas.